ROCKET BLUES

David Skuy

Scholastic Canada Ltd.

Toronto New York London Auckland Sydney
Mexico City New Delhi Hong Kong Buenos Aires

Scholastic Canada Ltd.
604 King Street West, Toronto, Ontario M5V 1E1, Canada
Scholastic Inc.
557 Broadway, New York, NY 10012, USA
Scholastic Australia Pty Limited
PO Box 579, Gosford, NSW 2250, Australia
Scholastic New Zealand Limited
Private Bag 94407, Botany, Manukau 2163, New Zealand
Scholastic Children's Books
Euston House, 24 Eversholt Street, London NW1 1DB, UK

www.scholastic.ca

Library and Archives Canada Cataloguing in Publication
Skuy, David, 1963-, author
      Rocket blues / David Skuy.
Issued in print and electronic formats.
ISBN 978-1-4431-3375-3 (pbk.)--ISBN 978-1-4431-3376-0 (html)
    I. Title.
PS8637.K72R62 2014   jC813'.6   C2014-901822-3
                                              C2014-901823-1

Cover photo © Gvictoria/Dreamstime.com

6 5 4 3 2 1   Printed in Canada 139   14 15 16 17 18

*To all the kids who ignore those who
tell them "no" and "you can't."*

CHAPTER 1

Rocket grabbed his hockey jacket and sticks and headed to the elevator. The TV was going full blast in apartment 1207. They drove his mom crazy because her bedroom was next to their living room. She'd asked them to turn it down lots of times, but nothing stopped them from watching at top volume. Now she just slept with earplugs. He pressed the elevator button. The hallway smelled different today — like moldy cheese — but underneath was its usual dusty smell. The guys in 1201 had dumped some garbage in the hall, but they were rough and there was no way anyone would tell them to clean it up.

When Rocket and his mom had first moved in, after his parents split up, she'd said the place was a dump and it would only be temporary: "A month at most." That was almost four years ago.

The elevator doors opened and Rocket stepped inside.

His thoughts turned to his team. Minor bantam this year — a huge step up for sure. He'd heard scouts came to games to check out guys for junior. Stupid that he had to bother with this tryout, though. The team was basically set. They only had to replace one kid, really — Derrick, the coach's son. He'd decided not to play competitive hockey this year. Rocket still found that hard to believe. Derrick was one of the best defencemen in the entire league.

He looked down at the crest on his jacket. His mom had sewed it on only two days before: *Oakmont Huskies AAA — Peewee Champions.* His chest filled with pride. What a team. Only lost one game all year, and that was in the playoffs. He'd centred the number one line with his two best buds, Ty and Adam, and he'd come within four points of setting a scoring record. The three friends had a favourite saying: "Bring it." That's what he was going to do this year. He could've gotten four more points. From now on he was going full out, every shift, every game. He gripped his sticks tightly.

Bring it.

And he would keep bringing it until he made the NHL.

The doors opened at the ground floor.

"Hey, where you going? Hockey?"

"What was your first clue?" He grinned at his friend Maddy and stepped out.

"Didn't you just finish the season or something?" she said.

"That was the playoffs. This is a tryout. You have tryouts in April for the next season, which starts in September," he said.

"So do I get a break from having to listen to you talk about hockey after your tryouts?" Maddy said. She straightened her arms out, pulled the ratty cuffs of her sweater down to cover her hands, and crossed her arms. She looked pale and tired today, probably from too much studying. She was always working on something for school.

"Well . . . there are usually three tryouts, although the team is basically the same as last season, so the next two are more like practices. Then we usually do a tournament or two, plus we continue our land training, and I'm playing in the three-on-three league with Ty and Adam, so . . . not too much more."

"Awesome," she said, clapping her hands. "There are two hours in August when you won't irritate me about your hockey."

"I'll always irritate you about something," he laughed.

She brushed a strand of hair from her face and tucked it behind her ear. She looked the same as always: grey wool sweater that was way too big for her, jeans with rips at the bottom, black boots laced up and her hair tied in a ponytail. "You don't *always* irritate me — just most of the time," she said.

He knew she was joking and he laughed again. Maddy was one of his best friends, even though they went to different schools. Her school was just around the corner, but his mom had wanted him to go to one in a better district. She'd gotten him on a waiting list for Forest Mills, called the principal about a thousand times, and talked to a bunch of teachers. He was pretty sure she'd even lied — saying they were looking to move into the neighbourhood, when there was no way they could ever afford to. It was a seriously rich area.

Rocket had met Maddy when he'd moved into the

building, and she was always around. She ended up hanging at his place most nights, either for dinner or to watch TV or to game. He probably spent more time with her than Ty and Adam.

"You coming or going?" he said.

"Coming. Griffen needed me to buy him some Advil. He's home early from work with a headache — probably self-inflicted at the bar last night. He's being such a jerk."

"That's what Griffens do." Rocket grinned.

"This time he's setting a Griffen record for jerkiness," Maddy said.

Griffen was her mom's boyfriend — or, more like, ex-boyfriend. Maddy's mom had taken off with some other guy a year ago and had never come back. Maddy didn't have anyone else, so she'd been living with Griffen since then. Rocket felt so bad for her. Griffen was about his least favourite person in the world.

"Hey, do you want to do something later?" Maddy asked.

"I think I'm going over to Ty's after the tryout," he said. "He got this amazing new hockey game for his Xbox."

She shrugged. "No problem. I have homework."

She always seemed to be doing homework. "You should do something fun for a change."

Maddy looked into his eyes. He felt a chill. Her eyes were fixed and hard, her lips pressed tightly together — and then, just like that, her face relaxed and she laughed. "I forgot, you've never heard of homework. Sorry. I'll explain how it works sometime."

He laughed and tapped the floor with his sticks.

"Looking forward to learning about this ho . . . me . . . wor . . . k?" he said very slowly.

She smirked and pressed the elevator button. He headed to the front door.

"There's more to life than hockey," she called out.

He shook his sticks in the air and, without turning around, said, "You're the funniest person I know. See ya."

"Bye, Bryan."

Her voice sounded kind of strange, and he almost turned around. But that was classic Maddy. Laughing one second, deadly serious the next, and then back to laughing. Probably just a bad day at school; maybe she only got a 95 on her math test.

"Hi, Bryan," a man called out.

"Hi, Grady," Rocket said.

A shabbily dressed man was squatting against the wall beside the lobby doors. His sleeping bag was pushed up against the building, his shopping cart lying on its side on the walkway.

"Got a hockey game?" he asked Rocket.

"I do, Grady," he replied.

"I used to play hockey — a right-winger. Played junior. I could've gone pro, too, if I hadn't messed my knee up. I could've," Grady said. He shook his head.

"I bet. Too bad about the knee," Rocket said.

"Played in Springfield. Nice people there. They loved me. Coach's name was . . ." He growled and shook his head. "Can't remember."

"Gotta run. See ya, Grady," Rocket said.

Grady tipped an imaginary hat at him. Rocket set off for the bus stop.

Most nights Grady slept in the alleyway beside the

apartment building. Once in a while, a cop would chase him away, but he always came back. Every time he saw Rocket carrying his hockey sticks he'd tell him he used to play — usually on a different team and with a different coach. It was kind of funny and sad at the same time. This wasn't the first time he'd mentioned Springfield, though. He must have been a fan. There used to be a famous team called the Springfield Indians that started way back in the 1920s or '30s. They'd had a coach, a guy named Eddie Shore, who was a Hall of Famer and had played with the Bruins.

Rocket began to walk faster. This wasn't sports trivia time. This was the time to get pumped. Sure, it was only a tryout; but they had a new coach, a guy named Barker. He was going to be paid, not like Derrick's dad, Coach Neilson, who'd done it for fun. First impressions were huge. Rocket needed to establish his rep as first-line centre.

Go hard every drill.

His mom wasn't thrilled about a paid coach. She thought it meant the fees would go up, and it was already expensive. He couldn't stop himself from sighing. He probably wouldn't need new pads this year. Why was he the only kid who wasn't growing? Next to Ty and Adam, he looked like the kid brother. Some guys in the league were almost a head taller than him. He took vitamins, got lots of sleep and didn't eat junk food: all the things the doctor told him to do. Nothing helped.

The bus was coming, and he ran the last little bit. Two other guys arrived at the same time and stepped in front of him. Rocket looked away, backing up to give them some room. They wore gang colours. You didn't mess with guys like that. The doors of the bus opened and people started to get on.

The line slowed.

"Push on," one of the guys in front of him said, "or I'll throw you off."

People pushed their way forward. The bottom step opened up and the two guys jumped on.

"Excuse me," Rocket said. "Can I slip on too? I'm meeting some people and . . ."

One of the guys ignored him. The other snickered.

"What's your problem, little man?"

"Uh, nothing," Rocket stammered. He hated this neighbourhood.

A man behind Rocket muttered something under his breath and went to sit in the bus shelter. The doors closed and the bus pulled away.

Ty's dad got annoyed when he was late for pickup. The next bus would be at least fifteen minutes. If his mom only had a car like everyone else . . . He kicked his bag. She didn't, and that was that.

It was embarrassing having to get a lift all the time.

He spun his bag sideways and sat down, right in front of the stop. He was going to be the first one on the next bus, even if he had to cross-check someone, and he didn't care what gang they belonged to.

One day he'd teach guys like that not to disrespect the Rocket.

One day.

CHAPTER 2

The puck caromed off the boards, spinning like a top near centre. Ty and Rocket turned toward it.

"All yours, Rocket. Set it up," Ty said.

"Go wide right," Rocket said. He pulled the puck onto his forehand with the tip of his stick and shovelled it back to his left defenceman, who fired it across ice to his partner, who one-timed it to Adam. Rocket had timed his curl perfectly and was across his own blue line, shoulders squared, when the puck hit Adam's stick.

"Ad-man!" he called.

He took Adam's pass without breaking stride. Coach Neilson would have loved that play. They'd worked on it all last season.

Ty had set up on the right side, just across centre. Rocket sent the puck over, confident Ty would know what to do. Sure enough, half a metre before Rocket hit the blue line, the puck lofted into the corner of the red team's zone. Rocket raced past the defenceman and gathered it in, cradling the puck on his backhand, surveying the action.

The right defenceman lumbered toward him. Ty

stormed the net, covered by the left defenceman. Rocket almost laughed out loud.

It was going to be that easy.

They'd left Adam wide open. He waited another second to draw the reckless defenceman closer and saucered a soft pass into the high slot. Adam bore in on the goalie.

"Bring it!" Rocket yelled.

Ty set up a screen and Adam cut to his left to give himself a shooting lane. He had the best shot on the team. Rocket knew he'd score; he never missed from there.

Suddenly, Rocket was flat on his back and sliding to the wall. The defenceman had extended his gloves into Rocket's chest and carried through with his shoulder.

"You've gotta be kidding!" Rocket said, scrambling to his feet.

This guy was toast — who cheap-shots the first-line centre? Seriously. His teammates would kill him.

At the blue line, Adam was punching gloves with Ty and the two defencemen. He'd obviously scored, which meant they hadn't seen the hit. Rocket took a step forward and then hesitated. The defenceman had already turned away. But that wasn't what made him stop. He was the biggest player on the ice — huge. Rocket barely came up to his chest.

He decided to let it go. The defenceman couldn't skate and he was useless with the puck — the type of guy who comes to a AAA tryout so he can brag about it to his friends. A tourist. He'd be cut and that would be the end of it. No point fighting. Rocket skated to his linemates, his glove extended. He looked back at the defenceman. How could a thirteen-year-old be so big?

"Did you see that ape run me over?" Rocket said, as he punched Adam's glove.

"I was too busy dangling that pathetic goalie," Adam said. "Has he even played before? I almost didn't know where to shoot, I saw so much net."

"Barker wants a change," Ty said.

"Doesn't want us to make the Red team look too bad," Adam said.

Rocket laughed. He followed Ty and Adam to the bench.

The tryout had been a total snore so far. They'd done a ton of skating drills and then they'd gone in alone on the goalies. Barker had finally blown the whistle and organized everyone into two teams for a scrimmage. There were so many guys that Rocket had only had two shifts.

If Rocket was unimpressed by the tryout, he was even less impressed by their new coach. When Barker wasn't talking to the other assistant coaches or the team sponsor, he was screaming at kids like a maniac, telling them to "want it" and to "push through the wall." One kid had fumbled a pass and Barker had called him useless. Maybe the kid didn't have the skills, but that was harsh.

Rocket had to go behind the bench and sidestep his way to the middle to find a place to sit. The bench was totally packed.

Ty and Adam were sitting together.

He tapped their helmets. "Hey, move over — if you get called bench hogs, it won't be my fault."

Ty snorted. "I can live with it."

"No room, bro. Suck it up," Adam said. He turned and grinned up at Rocket.

Rocket was irritated, but he let it go. It *was* crowded and it wouldn't kill him to stand. But he wasn't going to let them burn him just like that. He reached forward to grab a water bottle, smacking Ty and Adam on their helmets with his elbow.

"You're going to hurt for that," Ty said.

"Suck it up, bros," he said, taking a sip of water.

Adam elbowed Ty. "Bark-Breath alert."

Adam was always coming up with nicknames. He'd given new handles to half the kids on the team, including himself, Rocket and Ty, whose real name was Tyler.

Barker leaned sideways against the boards and draped an arm over the lip. "Love the drive to the net, Tyler," Barker said. "Strong net presence. And way to keep your head up, Adam: great skill move to pop it in."

"Thanks, Coach," Ty and Adam said.

Barker lowered his head. "We'll be making tons of cuts," he said quietly. "I thought it was dumb to have an open tryout for a AAA team — I think our sponsor likes the money everyone pays." He laughed. "Tomorrow will be more like a real practice. I've made my decisions already." He gave Ty and Adam's gloves a punch and skated away.

Rocket took a sip of water. Barker probably hadn't noticed him standing behind the bench. Nice of him to forget who set the goal up, though.

Whatever.

Rocket had a feeling he was going to miss Coach Neilson. He never would've talked about other players like that. It was also kind of weird to hear Barker trash-talk the sponsor. Rocket took another sip of water. Next shift he'd make that ape of a defenceman pay for his late hit. He'd wait until he wasn't looking and then pop him under the chin, real quick. The dude was too slow to ever catch him. He'd only got that hit in because Rocket had been caught watching the play.

Coach Neilson had been on him about that, too. Don't watch the puck — skate!

There was always something to work on in hockey. Like Coach Neilson said, even professionals practise.

The whistle blew, and Barker waved them to centre.

Rocket hit the bench with his stick.

"No way that's the end of the scrimmage," he said. "We got on twice, for like a minute. Worst tryout ever."

"Doesn't matter," Ty said to him. "You heard him. They're going to cut everyone and we can have a real practice tomorrow."

Rocket shrugged. "Still, it's an hour and a half of ice wasted. Kind of pointless."

"Hey, we popped one in," Adam said, "so it wasn't totally a waste."

He put a skate on the bench then threw his legs over the boards. Ty laughed and did the same.

Rocket grimaced and walked to the door. The showing off was getting on his nerves — big time. So what if they could hop over the boards.

He shuffled out and drifted to centre where Barker had set up with the players around him in a semi-circle.

Rocket felt sorry for the new guys that had come out. Brutal to kill yourself trying to impress a coach who couldn't even be bothered to run a real tryout. He wasn't even watching half the time — more than half — and each player had to pay thirty bucks!

"Great work. Good energy," Barker said. "Thanks for coming out. I hope you appreciate a real, top-level tryout and get a feel for what it takes to play with the best. The Oakmont Huskies might be too much of a jump for some of you, but I admire your guts for coming anyway. Hope you had fun. As the saying goes, many are called, few are chosen. That's a life lesson, boys. We can only carry fifteen skaters, with two goalies. Good luck with any other tryouts and, hopefully, I'll run into you again." He paused. "So, guys, that was awesome. Now, let's go for a skate three times around the rink to end it off. Go for it — I'll be watching." He blasted his whistle.

The boys took off. The players who'd been on the Huskies last year lazed along, including Ty and Adam. Rocket skated up beside them.

"Come on," he said. "Let's go for a skate."

"Too pathetic," Adam said. "No point busting our butts for nothing. Look at them. Don't they get it?"

The other guys were skating their hearts out, and soon a few had even lapped them.

Barker was off the ice by now, speaking to the team manager, Rob Thompson, and the sponsor, Mr. Cole. The sponsor's son Sean played on the team. Adam called him Money, on account of his rich dad.

Money wasn't Rocket's favourite guy: he was always bragging about the awesome trips he was going on or the new, expensive things his dad had bought him. Rocket knew some rich kids at Forest Mills, but they were nothing compared to Money's dad, apparently. He was some kind of lawyer.

At least Money could play. Rob's son, Mitchell, was totally useless. He barely got any ice time, but he was still on the team.

Another pack of guys lapped them. Rocket couldn't stand it.

"Let's show them how Huskies skate," Rocket said. "We look like house leaguers."

"I can't be seen sweating at a tryout," Adam cracked.

"Go for it, Rocket," Ty said. "We'll clap for you."

Rocket snickered. "If you can't keep up, I understand." He took off.

Ty took off after him.

The two boys motored around the ice, weaving in and out of the other players. Rocket carved sharply on his inside edges, the blades scraping over the ice as he swung around the net. A few short, powerful strides and he was back at top speed. Ty still hadn't caught him — and he wasn't going to. He wasn't called the Rocket for nothing. He swerved to the middle of the ice to avoid a pack of players, and with arms and legs pumping faster and faster, he felt like he was practically flying.

He wished the tryout was just beginning.

A whistle blew. "That's it, boys. Clear off. Zamboni's coming on." Rob waved at them from the door. Rocket figured he could sneak in another lap, and with no one in his way, he went even faster. Ty and Adam were still on the ice talking to Rob when he rounded the last corner. He skidded to a stop a metre away, spraying them with ice chips.

"Sorry, Ty. Thought you were a pylon," Rocket said.

Ty rubbed the top of Rocket's helmet. "How cute. The little boy wants to play."

Rocket knew Ty wasn't serious. It still bothered him, though.

"Must've been hard to watch someone's back in a race," Rocket said.

"I got no problem losing to you," Ty said, tapping his shin pads. "So did you see anyone you liked?"

They stepped off the ice and headed to the dressing room. Rocket felt dumb getting mad at Ty for making a stupid joke. They were best friends!

"Hard to tell with so many guys," Rocket said. "There was that left-winger in the blue helmet and the red pants. He looked like a player."

Ty shrugged. "Bit small, especially for a winger. I bet that huge defenceman will make it. He could clear the front of the net with his pinky finger."

Rocket flushed as he opened the door to the dressing room. Hockey was about heart and skill, not stupid muscle.

"Awesome skate, Tyler," Barker called out. "Great sniping, Ad-man."

The dressing room door closed behind them.

CHAPTER 3

The players from last season had basically taken over one of the dressing rooms. It was like last season hadn't ended. Craig was kneeling in the middle of the room undoing his goalie pads. Bennett and Jerrett were having their usual burping competition, which was way better than what they sometimes did. Joshua was trying to balance a shin pad on his head, and Money was yapping away — this time about Barker.

"He played in the East Coast League," Money was saying. "And I think he played in Europe, too, in Italy, or something like that. Dude is going to be awesome. Dad says Neilson was too soft. Barker's going to make this team a legend. We're probably going to Europe for a tourney, because he knows guys over there. We're adding another practice each week and land training — he says we aren't in shape."

A quiet murmur spread through the room.

"That'll be awesome," Adam said to Rocket and Ty. "We'll take over Europe."

Rocket wasn't so sure. "Sounds crazy expensive. We did like six or seven tournaments last year. Isn't that enough?" His knew his mom couldn't afford any more.

"Money's dad will pay," Adam scoffed. "He's worth millions. It's world domination time, bros. I'm totally pumped about minor bantam."

"Yeah, sure. It'll be fun, but—"

Adam cut Rocket off. "My dad said junior teams will be scouting us; even college teams begin to notice you. We have the same season as last year and it'll be the big time."

"Bring it," Ty said.

"Bring it," Rocket said with energy. He meant it, too. Coach Neilson had pulled him aside after they'd won the championship and told him he was a special player, a kid who had a chance to make it if he worked hard and dedicated himself. Bryan Rockwood wasn't afraid of hard work: hours spent shooting tennis balls against the garbage bin behind his apartment, shinny on Ty's backyard rink in the winter, floor hockey at school, hockey camps every summer, the three-on-three league. His entire life was hockey — just the way he liked it.

The door swung open and Rob came in.

"Hi, Uncle Robby," the boys chorused — another one of Adam's nicknames.

Usually, Rob laughed at that. Now he looked deadly serious. Rocket stuffed his hockey pants into his bag. Rob held up his clipboard.

"Okay, boys. Listen up. I'm going to read off some names. If I call your name, please stay in this room. If I don't call your name, please go to dressing room one or two. Okay?" Rob looked around.

His face was pale. Rocket wondered if he was sick.

The room quieted down. Rocket's chest tightened.

No matter what, he always felt nervous when cuts were made. He felt bad for the guys who didn't make it.

"Bennett, Michael, Sean, Joshua . . ."

Rocket wiped his skate blades.

"Adam, Tyler, Craig, Mitchell . . ."

Rocket put his skates in his bag.

"Harrison, Christopher, Jerrett . . ."

Jerrett was the assistant coach's son. Better than Mitchell, but not by much. Rocket tried to catch Ty's eye, but he wasn't looking his way.

"Nicholas, Ryan, Simon and Brett."

Rob lowered his clipboard. "That's it. If I didn't call your name, you can haul your stuff outside when you're done dressing. You can give it to your parents or take it into room one or two." He nodded several times, his eyes wide.

No one said a word. Rocket thought his chest was going to burst open. He gathered his courage. "You didn't call me," he said finally.

Rob tapped his clipboard with a pen. "Coach Barker will talk to you in one of the other dressing rooms and explain how things will work this year. Okay? So hustle it up if I didn't call you, and . . . yeah . . . That's it. Just hustle it up 'cause a couple of other boys need to come in here." He left.

Rocket zipped his bag shut. Adam was rubbing his skate blades over and over with a towel.

"Probably no big deal," Ty whispered. "I bet Barker is going to ask you to switch positions or lines or something."

"Our line led the league in scoring last season," Rocket whispered back. "Why would he mess that up?"

Ty shook his head and shrugged. Adam was still drying his skates. Without knowing what else to do, Rocket got up, grabbed his sticks and pulled his bag to the door as it swung open. It was the huge defenceman who'd decked him.

"S'cuse me, broski," the defenceman said.

He held the door open and Rocket had no choice but to walk under his arm to get out. Another kid pushed past Rocket on his way in.

"After you," Rocket said. The kid ignored him. Inside, the guys began talking at once. The door closed before he heard what they were saying.

A bunch of parents had gathered outside the door. Money's dad had his arm around Barker's shoulders and they were both laughing. Rocket dragged his bag into dressing room two.

Everyone there had changed into their clothes. Most had their feet on their bags and were leaning against the wall. With nowhere to sit, Rocket pushed his bag to the side and tried to look chill. He had a feeling he wasn't doing a good job of it. His insides were churning, and he felt sick to his stomach. He'd centred Ty and Adam for three years; he'd always been a centre. He didn't want to have to learn a new position. He shot left, so was Barker going to move Adam to centre? That made no sense. If anything, Ty would be the better centre — more of an all-around player.

A few of the boys were outright staring at him. Out of the corner of his eye, he noticed the winger with the blue helmet and red pants.

Barker barged in. "Listen up, boys," he said, banging a clipboard on his thigh. "I always do this myself. I think it's the right thing to do. I'm a straight shooter, always have been. So here's the deal. We won't be able to offer you guys a spot this year on the Huskies. Sorry. Like I said on the ice, and as most of you know, the Huskies are the best AAA team in the league. No shame in not making it. None. Good luck with your other try-outs — and thanks again." He turned and reached for the door.

Rocket raced over.

"Coach?" Rocket said. He hated that his voice shook.

Barker's eyes narrowed. "I have to speak to my team. Thanks for coming."

He pushed the door open and went out.

Rocket followed. He heard a few guys laugh — probably at him — but he didn't care. What was happening?

He tugged on Barker's jacket before he went into the Huskies dressing room.

"I'm Bryan Rockwood — Rocket, at least the guys call me that. It's not my real name." His throat had gone completely dry, he was so nervous. "Anyway, I was on the team last year — the last three years."

Barker put his hand on Rocket's shoulder. "There was a lot of talent on the ice and I had to make some tough decisions. That's hockey. Good luck to you." He turned away and Rocket reached out again.

"But I was leading scorer last year. I was centre on a line with Ty and Ad-man . . . I mean, Tyler and Adam. I've always played with them — centre, I mean." His voice broke. He was on the edge of losing it. "All my friends . . ."

Barker bit his lower lip and he rubbed his hands together. "I'm a straight shooter, like I said. Ask anyone. I'm honest as the day is long and I'm going to be honest with you. No point beating around the bush. Sure you can play. Yeah, you got good wheels, and maybe even a little jam. Only there's something you don't got — and there's nothing you can do about it." He held his hand over Rocket's head. "Size. You're too small. My teams play tough and physical. I need big bodies that can cycle and crash the net, not fancy skaters that play outside. You've had a few years at AAA, and on the Huskies to boot. Lots of good memories. But that's over. Trust me, I'm doing you a favour. Before you get your head taken off, go down to AA, or even A. Have some fun; don't take hockey so seriously. It's too physical at this level for someone your size. Sorry to be the guy to tell you; that's just me. I don't like to lead kids on. You'll thank me one day for telling you the truth. Trust me. It just isn't going to happen for you."

Barker pushed the door open.

Rocket remained frozen.

Cut!

The perfect word.

That's how he felt, like someone had cut his heart out. After everything, all the practices, the working out, the championship, the trophies, it was all over — after one stupid tryout. Just like that.

Fifteen minutes ago he was the Rocket, AAA hockey player.

Now who was he?

A cheer sounded from inside the dressing room.

CHAPTER 4

Ty's father, Greg, reached for Rocket's hockey bag. "Give it here, Bryan. I'll toss it in the trunk."

"I can do it," Rocket said. He heaved his bag beside Ty's.

Adam's father came over. "Greg, looks like an awesome crew!" he said.

"Hey, Rod. Yeah, I guess. I'm dropping Bryan off first, so . . . we can talk later," Greg said.

Rod's grin became strained. "I didn't see you there, Rocket. Sorry, buddy. Tough break, real tough. Game is getting rougher, though. Boys are growing; they start hitting for real now. Probably for the best, right? No sense getting hammered on the ice by a kid twice your size."

Rocket stared at the trunk, his hands stuffed in his jacket.

Rod began to laugh. "At least your jacket will last for a few years. The way Adam's going he'll be out of it by the summer."

Greg slammed the trunk shut. "We really have to go . . . so . . . Take care."

"See you, Ad-man," Ty said.

Adam flicked his head. "Catch ya later, bros. Bring it!"

Rocket pulled on the door handle, but the angle was bad and the latch caught.

"Here, I'll do it," Ty said.

"I can open a stupid door," Rocket said. He pulled harder and the door flew open and slammed against the stopper. Just before he climbed in, he saw Greg whisper something to Rod, who nodded back. Ty followed him in, and soon Greg got behind the wheel and began to reverse out of the parking spot.

"I'll try to speak to Coach Barker," Greg said over his shoulder. "Not sure he's the listening type, unfortunately. For the record, I think it was a bad decision, Bryan. Terrible. I'd have you on the team if it was up to me."

Rocket knew he should say thank you. The words just wouldn't come out.

"Maybe if your mom called Rob or Money's dad?" Ty said.

"Doubt it. She doesn't know them. Besides, Barker hates me; he won't change his mind," Rocket said.

"There will be lots of teams dying to have you," Greg said. "I'll make some calls when I get home, okay? Let me see what's available. I know most of the coaches. The only problem is a lot of the better clubs will have their rosters full already, but you never know. How does that sound?"

He wasn't actually sure. "Depends where they practise," he said. "I'd need a new carpool, since we still don't have a car . . ." His voice trailed off.

"You're a skilled player," Greg said. "Sure, you're on the small side, but look at the NHL. Lots of small guys make it. Who's the guy . . . you know . . . won a scoring title, has a French-sounding name? C'mon. It's on the tip of my tongue. Who was it?"

"Martin St. Louis?" Rocket offered.

"That's it. St. Louis. Maybe he's an exception, but still . . . Anyway, why are we talking about the NHL? You're playing for fun, so what's the big deal? We'll miss you on the team, though, and I know Ty and Adam are disappointed. Right, Ty?"

"Absolutely."

"But you'll find another team and have fun, too. Right?" Greg said.

Rocket wanted to jump out the window. He didn't eat right and train and practise for hours because hockey was just for *fun*. No one took him seriously because they thought he was too puny. And if one more person mentioned Martin St. Louis — or Theo Fleury — he was going to kill them!

Greg continued in a strained voice. "You boys play so much hockey; it might be good to think of other things, too. When one door closes another opens up, as they say. I've been after Ty to expand his interests, try new things. There's more to life than rinks and slapshots."

"Here comes the lecture about being a well-rounded kid," Ty said.

Greg laughed good-naturedly. "I didn't have your talent when I was a kid, so I know it's different for you boys. I was a total hack. I get that you love playing because you're so good at it. Still . . . and be honest,

Bryan, don't you ever get bored with hockey?" Greg said.

Rocket wanted to yell "No!"

Instead, he shrugged and said, "Maybe."

"So what else do you do besides hockey?" Greg said.

"Lots of stuff, I guess." That wasn't really true. Other than TV, the computer and school, hockey was about it. That's who he was — a hockey player. Everyone at school knew him for hockey, plus all of his friends and family — even Grady.

"Great," Greg said. "Maybe this is an opportunity to make hockey part of your life instead of your entire life. I'm even jealous a bit. This Barker's got us playing all over the place. Ty, did you hear about the Europe tour?"

"Money told us about it," Ty said.

"This team sure digs into my pocketbook," Greg chuckled. "Every time there's a fundraiser it costs me about five hundred bucks! It'll be a great experience, of course. The boys must've gone nuts when Coach Barker announced it."

"We're pumped," Ty said.

Rocket felt sick. No Europe for him. He was headed to Loserville.

Greg's phone rang and he stuck a Bluetooth receiver in his ear.

"Hey, Rod . . . Yup, the talent level is high, through the roof, for sure . . . Size is definitely . . ." He paused. "Yep, we can ramp up the physical game."

Rocket tried to tune out the conversation. He couldn't think of anything to say to Ty, though, which was weird because their teachers were always telling them to be quiet. Ty had mentioned hanging out after the tryout, but all Rocket wanted to do was go home. Ty didn't bring it up either. He was quiet, too.

After what felt like forever, they pulled up in front of Rocket's apartment building. Greg popped the trunk.

"Hold on a sec, I'm dropping Bryan off." Greg muted the phone. "Bryan, you should probably take your bag this time. You'll be going to other tryouts and . . . you'll obviously need it," he said.

"Okay."

"Ty, help Rocket with his bag."

"I can do it," Rocket said. "I'm not that small."

Greg laughed loudly. "Glad to see you're keeping your sense of humour about this, Bryan. Like I said, I'll phone around. There's bound to be something."

Rocket didn't remember making a joke. He hauled his bag out and reached for his sticks.

"Speak to you soon," Greg said.

"Bye," Ty said.

Rocket closed the trunk. He watched the van pull away. It turned at the lights and disappeared from view. He'd been so pumped all day. A few hours ago he was the happiest kid in the world, skating with guys he thought would be his buds forever. Now everything had changed.

He looked up at his building. Sadly, it was the same. The white bricks still looked dingy, like someone had poured a huge cup of coffee over the entire place. There was garbage everywhere. One of the windows in the lobby door was boarded up and Grady was sleeping in the alley. The scene made the hurt in his heart worse.

Rocket wheeled his bag into the lobby. He had no idea where he'd store his stuff. He'd always left it at Ty's. His dad had even built a small room downstairs for the equipment, with dummies to dry stuff out.

He stopped, closed his eyes and took a deep breath. This was like a bad shift, he told himself. It was over, done with. Flush it, as Coach Neilson used to say. Greg would find him a team, and then he'd show that Barker. He'd show them all — Money, Craig, Jerrett, Joshua — all of them. Barker was an idiot, and there were lots of good teams — the Thunder, the Rangers, the Kings, the Sharks, the Nats. Let's see what the Huskies would do without him, without their lead scorer.

And how awesome would it be when his new team kicked their butts. He'd have the last laugh at Bark-Breath — and Rob and Money's dad — and Greg and Rod — and Ty and Adam, too.

Too small?

Not this Rocket!

CHAPTER 5

He dropped his equipment in the living room. He'd figure out where to put it later.

"Hey, how's it going?" Maddy asked.

"Maddy? What are you doing here?"

He walked into the kitchen. She closed the laptop.

"I didn't feel like hanging with Griffen, so I called your mom and asked if I could stay here."

He shrugged, but it was the last thing he wanted. He could use some alone time.

"She should be home in a sec," Maddy said cheerfully. "She just called: said she was around the corner. I'm surprised you didn't see her when you came up."

He nodded.

"I thought you were going to Ty's to play on his awesome Xbox and do all sorts of awesome stuff at his awesome house?"

"Nope."

Her mouth opened slightly. "Okay," she said finally. "You want to . . . Hey, your mom said there was chicken in the fridge for your dinner. Are you hungry?" She sniffed the air. "What's that smell?"

"Nothing."

He so wanted her to leave.

The door opened.

He crossed his arms and closed his eyes and leaned against the wall.

"You're home! Maddy thought you were going over to Ty's. Do you want dinner?" his mom asked. He shook his head. She put an arm around his shoulders and kissed him on the head. "Okay, and let's not be shy about a shower," she said. "You really have a hockey smell on you today."

"It's not me," he snapped. "I barely worked up a sweat. There were fifty guys on the ice, at least. Played two shifts in a scrimmage and that's it."

She sniffed the air. "Something smells funky."

"I smell it, too," Maddy said.

He rolled his neck. They were so irritating.

"I wonder if it's the garbage?" his mom said.

"It's my stupid hockey bag!" he yelled.

His mom, wide-eyed, was clearly not impressed.

"When did you decide that kind of behaviour was acceptable?" she said.

"Well . . . it's like . . . the smell is the most important thing in the world . . . It's kind of annoying. Sorry," he managed.

His mom opened the fridge. "Are you sure you wouldn't like something to eat?" she said. "Are you hungry, Maddy?"

"Maybe a little," she said.

"Didn't you eat dinner?"

Maddy shrugged. "I wasn't that hungry."

His mom took two Tupperware containers from the

fridge. "You know you can help yourself anytime, Maddy. Now I feel bad thinking you've been sitting here hungry all this time."

"I really wasn't hungry," Maddy said.

"Nonsense," his mom said. "Can you get two plates, Bryan? And some glasses — and heck, why not some cutlery?"

She laughed.

Rocket growled and kicked at the floor.

His mom's smile faded. "You're not making this the most pleasant moment in my life," she said to him.

"Aren't you even going to ask about the tryout, or why the hockey bag's here?"

He couldn't believe how little they cared.

His mom sighed. "Bryan, I've just finished a twelve-hour shift at the group home. One kid with autism ran away and for two hours we couldn't find him. Another kid told me he's depressed and doesn't want to get out of bed. So excuse me if I didn't walk in the door and immediately ask about your tryout. I'm not asking for a lot of slack, but a tiny bit would be nice."

"That's what you always say: 'Cut me some slack, cut me some slack.' Cut *me* some slack, why don't you?"

His mother folded her hands across her chest. Her eyes were red, and they had big bags under them. The laugh lines on her cheeks seemed deeper than normal.

"Okay, Bryan," she said softly. "I'm sorry. What's wrong with the Huskies?"

He suddenly remembered he was still wearing his Huskies jacket. He let it slip off and fall to the floor.

"Can you at least hang that up?" his mom said wearily.

"I'm going to throw it out," he said.

She didn't respond.

"I got cut," he blurted.

She put a hand to her mouth. "But . . . how? You were . . . You're on the team, I thought. This seems totally last second."

Rocket's stomach felt hard and tight, like he'd eaten a rock. "This was the tryout for next season. I wasn't actually on the team — just assumed I was."

"Bryan . . ." She looked at him in wonder. "You did so well last year. What happened? Did you get nervous? I could talk to the coach."

"I didn't get nervous," he groaned. "There's a new coach, this idiot named Barker. He played in the East Coast League, and in Italy or something, and he acts like such a big deal. Yells at guys all the time and says they suck and stuff, and all he cares about is size. If you're big, you're in." He had to stop for a second to calm down. He had a big lump in his throat. "He cut me in front of everyone, in the dressing room, in front of Ty and Adam and — everyone. They read the names out, one at a time, and they didn't call me. I had to walk out with everyone laughing at me and . . . and . . ." He couldn't finish.

"Are you sure that's the reason?" his mom said quietly.

"Barker told me I was too small, Mom. I asked him. He said he wants big guys. He even kept this useless defenceman because he's big. I totally smoked the guy in the scrimmage, and set up Adam for a goal, but I got cut and he made it."

She ran a hand through her hair. "That's so unfair," she said. She sounded upset. "You've been on the team for three years. I'm going to speak to the coach, this Barker fellow, and give him a piece of my mind. It's ridiculous to pick a team based solely on size."

"Don't call! Please? He won't listen. Trust me. He's like a wall and he won't care what you think."

"Is there a chance some guys will drop out and you can get back on?" Maddy said.

He threw his hands up. "It doesn't work that way! Guys don't just *drop out*. This is the Huskies — best team in the league. Drop out and play for who?" He glared at her.

Maddy looked over at his mom.

"We can talk about this later," his mom said. "I can imagine this is a shock and it's very upsetting. I know this was very important to you. And . . . I'm a bit in a shock, too. You played for the Huskies for three years . . . and all the money I gave them . . . ridiculous. Every year it gets more expensive, too. Anyway, let's eat and forget about the Huskies."

"First we need to call the Thunder and the Rangers — and the Kings, and the Sharks, and the Nats," Rocket said. "They're probably making offers tonight. They need to know I'm available. All the spots will be gone. Ty's dad said he'd call some people, but who knows if he will."

"Hang up your coat and you can eat something. We can deal with this tomorrow," his mother said. "I'm exhausted."

"You have to call now, seriously, or I won't have a team this season. Spots go unbelievably fast."

"One night won't matter, Bryan. It's almost nine o'clock."

His head was going to explode. "Tomorrow is too late. I need you to do this. I can't call. I'm a kid. They won't talk to me. You have to. That's what real parents do. They get their kids onto good teams. Jerrett's and Mitchell's dads are coaches, Money's dad is a sponsor and Greg and Rod come to all the games — but you barely even see me play. You don't get it!"

"Enough!" Her eyes flashed. "I have to work shifts at the group home, but I've seen you play plenty — I've frozen in more rinks that I can remember. Your dad can be an assistant coach if he wants. I'm not the hockey fan in the family."

"So now it's dad's fault? He lives too far away."

She slammed her hand on the counter and Maddy jumped. "As usual, it's the awful mom's fault — the one who has a job and pays the bills. Who do you think pays for your hockey? Not your wonderful father who can't seem to keep a job or pay his child support."

"You haven't mentioned that today — a new record. Good job, Mom."

"And I could do without the sarcasm."

"I don't care!" Rocket shouted.

He stormed off. He gave his equipment a kick on the way to his bedroom, then slammed the door so loud the trophies on his shelf shook. The Huskies championship trophy sat on his desk. He squeezed past his bed and picked it up. The golden hockey player stared into space, posed gripping a stick. Rocket reared back to throw it at the wall.

Then he put it back on his desk. He'd earned it: Barker couldn't take that away. He sat down on his bed. His walls were covered in hockey posters. He'd strung a bunch of medals below the trophies on his shelf. His entire life was there, everything he'd ever done, everything important in his life. What did they mean now? Maybe he should throw them all out.

He looked at his trophies and medals for a while.

Guys get cut from teams all the time — or traded. Barker has his opinions. So what?

Rocket continued to stare.

But he *was* small. He was smaller than anyone else on the team.

What if Barker was right?

The front door closed. Maddy must have left. He'd acted like a jerk to his mom — he knew his dad wasn't really the best dad ever. Not even close. He maybe saw him once a month.

Still sitting, Rocket bounced on the bed a couple of times, the mattress squeaking each time. When he was a little kid, he used to bounce up and down for hours, even though his mom and dad begged him to stop. They had to buy him a new mattress when he was six because he'd trashed his old one. That seemed like a million years ago. He thought about what had happened since then: his parents fighting all the time and finally divorcing, moving out of their townhouse into this crappy apartment, saying goodbye to all his friends.

A wave of fear swept down his spine.

What if Barker was right?

What if Bryan Rockwood was too small to play competitive hockey?

There was a knock at the door, and then his mom came in. Rocket bounced softly on the bed and looked down at the floor.

"Sorry, Mom. I was mad about getting cut. I lost it. I'll say sorry to Maddy, too. I didn't mean it. Forget what I said."

He instantly felt better.

His mom sat next to him and began to rub his back. "It's okay, honey. I had a tough day at work and wasn't giving you the attention you deserved. That's not fair to you. I'm sorry, too." She paused, and with a twinkle in her eye, added, "My bad."

He tried not to laugh. "Kids don't really say that anymore."

She threw her hands up in the air. "Great. Just when I get cool you change the lingo on me."

Rocket pushed back against the wall. "The guy they kept, that defenceman, he's huge; I swear he's as big as Barker."

"I'm not sure I want you playing against someone that size," she said.

"I can take care of myself," he said. "I'm used to it. Why am I so small, though?" He squeezed his hands between his thighs. "It's so brutal seeing guys getting bigger and bigger, and I stay the same. I know you're not the tallest, but Dad's pretty big, and don't sons take after their fathers?"

"The doctor said there's nothing wrong with you. Your dad was small until he turned eighteen, and then he shot up six inches in one year."

"That'll be too late," he said sadly. "They draft when you're eighteen."

"Who does, dear?"

"Doesn't matter," he said.

He'd sound stupid if he told her the NHL.

She folded her hands on her lap. "So who did you want me to call, and how do we get the numbers?"

"You should call Greg," he said eagerly. "He knows all the teams. This'll be better, anyway. Barker was a jerk. Kept bragging about playing in the East Coast League — it's way lower than the AHL."

She smiled. "I'll take your word on that."

"And they want to do some stupid fancy Europe tour because Money's dad is such a big shot. They'll be fundraising all the time, and you hate that as much as me. I'll find another team, with a better coach." His eyes opened wide. "We should call Coach Neilson. I'm so stupid. He's totally connected. He'll know what to do."

"Okay. How about that shower?" she said.

"Sure. And you'll call Ty's dad and Coach Neilson?"

She tussled his hair. "Yes, Bryan."

"As in . . . now?"

She laughed and stood up. "I promise to call Greg and Coach Neilson immediately and get one Bryan 'The Rocket' Rockwood on the best team in the whole world."

"Awesome, Mom."

She opened the door.

"Hey, Mom . . . Thanks."

She closed her eyes briefly and then shook her head. "You don't have to thank me, honey. Happy to do it." She closed the door behind her.

His heart began to race. He needed to get pumped. He pictured Barker behind the bench, watching as he scored the winning goal to knock the Huskies out of the playoffs. Rocket let himself enjoy the image for a while. Then he hopped off the bed and began to do sit-ups. No more slacking off. He had to stick to his routine. The next few days were going to be totally intense: new team, new coaches, new players. He'd need to bring it, every play, every drill, every time he touched the puck, from the second his skates hit the ice.

This Rocket wasn't out of fuel — not even close.

CHAPTER 6

His mom slowed the car and turned left.

"There's a spot over there," Rocket said, "or you can just drop me off in front."

They cruised past a row of cars.

"Just park somewhere," he said, pressing against his seat in frustration. "We've gone around ten times. I'll miss the stupid tryout."

"Bryan, please relax. You've got plenty of time. There's a spot right there."

She pulled into it.

"For the record, this rink took us an hour to get to, and there was no traffic. Griffen can't lend us his car every time you play. If this is their home rink, I don't see how it'll work," she said.

"Griffen said it was no problem."

"We can't impose on him that much."

"I haven't even gotten out of the car and you're telling me I can't play?"

"I didn't say that, but I'm going to have to speak to the coach and find out if we can get into a carpool."

Rocket groaned. "This is my only option. The

Rangers, the Thunder and the Nats have no spots, the Kings said no, and the Sharks didn't even return our call. I don't want to play for the Wilmont Demons — we used to call them the Doorknobs — but they're my last chance."

His mother opened her door. "I'm only saying I have to speak to the coach. I didn't say you couldn't play. Let's not worry about the driving yet. We'll work it out. We always do." She blinked a few times. "Might be a good time for you to get your stuff and go."

"Good idea." He paused. "I'm kind of losing it, aren't I?"

"Sort of, but I know this is hard. We'll get through it." She squeezed his arm. "You better 'bring it' this tryout!"

"I got ya," he laughed.

He grabbed his equipment from the trunk, and they set off for the rink. The lobby was packed: hockey bags strewn about, groups of parents milling around the snack bar, kids running around. And, near the doors to the rink, there was a long white table with a man and a woman sitting behind it. Rocket felt a rush of nerves.

"Here's the twenty-five dollars," his mom said to him. "Can you register? I need a coffee."

He took the money. The line in front of the woman was shorter. He went behind a tall kid wearing a Dolphins jacket.

The woman asked for the boy's name.

"Duane Martins," he said.

"Position?"

"Right wing."

"Who'd you play for last year?"

He pointed to his jacket. "The Dolphins — AA."

Rocket figured she'd have a heart attack when she heard who he'd played for.

She gave Duane a red pinny and two sheets of paper with a number on each. He gave her the money and left.

"I'm sorry," the lady said to Rocket as he stepped forward. "This is the minor bantam tryout. The pee-wees tried out yesterday. I can give you the coach's number, although I think the team is full."

He felt himself go red in the face. "I'm here for the—"

"Phil, do you have Gord's number?" she said to the man beside her. "This little fellow got the wrong time and I thought he could call."

"That team's picked," Phil said. "Stayed with the same group of kids."

"I'm sorry, dear," she said to Rocket. "It's a hectic time of year. Are your parents here? I can explain the situation to them."

"I'm thirteen," he said. "I'm not out for peewee."

She gasped. "I'm sorry. Stupid of me. Some of the kids trying out are so big already, I just thought . . ." She leaned forward. "This is AAA, dear. It's very rough. Maybe you should stick to house league or something."

Rocket squeezed his fist in his pocket. "I'm Bryan Rockwood," he said between clenched teeth.

She hesitated, gave him a look and then wrote his name down. "It's twenty-five dollars for the tryout." He gave her the money. "And did you play last year?"

He'd been waiting for that. He took his time. "I did. I played for the AAA Oakmont Huskies."

She looked up from the paper. "Excuse me, Phil. This boy says he played for the Huskies last year."

"Did you play for Neilson?"

Rocket nodded.

"What did you say your name was?" Phil said.

"His name is Bryan Rockwood," the lady said.

Phil raised an eyebrow. "Why aren't you playing with the Huskies this year? I figured they'd be set."

Rocket's mind whirled. He should've figured out an answer for this. Of course, they'd ask. He couldn't tell the truth, and it wouldn't sound good if he bad-mouthed Barker.

"It was hard to get to the games — and they switched the practice rink. This would be more convenient." Dumbest reason ever. His mom would talk to the coach and he'd sound like an idiot.

It seemed to satisfy Phil, though. "Put him on Red. Have a good skate."

The lady handed him two pieces of paper — number 164. "Pin this to your pinny, front and back. We have dressing rooms five and six . . . and good luck."

Rocket turned to leave. A boy bumped into him. Rocket shot him an angry glance, but he didn't seem to care.

"Jeremy Burns," the boy announced.

"Hey, Jeremy, you ready to go hard?" said Phil.

Rocket took hold of his bag and sticks and hauled them through the doors. Duane was standing at the boards next to a man.

"Okay, bud, this is the Demons' third tryout," the man said to Duane. "Things are totally tight. I spoke to the coach. He said there were only two open spots. You have to want it more than the next kid, right? You got to be hungry. Get to every puck. Go hard every drill. I know you've been to a ton of tryouts, but we got the Aces offer out of it, at least. The Demons are AAA, though, and that's huge for you. Okay?"

"Okay, Dad," Duane said quietly.

Rocket continued along the boards to the dressing rooms. Duane's dad was right. Third tryouts were always tight. Of course, there'd only be a few spots. But they wouldn't have invited him to try out if there wasn't at least one forward spot left. If they already had three centres, he could always start at wing. They'd move him to the middle soon enough.

Dressing rooms five and six were at the far end. He glanced over at the ice. Some younger kids, probably minor peewee, were racing around. One player curled sharply to corral a bouncing puck near the boards at the red line. He was big. That was depressing — Rocket was even shorter than minor peewees!

His nerves kicked up, again. The rink had always been a familiar place: the echo of pucks off the boards, the whistle blasts, the shouts from coaches. It had been like a second home. It all felt different now, new, out of place, strange. He stopped in front of room five. The kids inside were pretty loud. He figured they were guys from last year. He went to room six. It was quiet — much better — a room where no one knew each other and he wouldn't stick out. He pushed the door open.

The faint murmur of conversation died out. Most of the boys were almost dressed, a few still taping their socks. No one seemed too interested in giving him a place to sit. He thought of going back to the other room, but he was scared of being in a room full of friends. He remembered last year's tryout when a new kid had come into their room and Money and Jerrett had him in tears in five minutes.

He spotted a bit of bench at the far end. He put his bag down in front of two guys.

"Can I squeeze in there?" he said.

A kid with dark, curly hair looked up. He wore a black pinny. "You sure you got the right tryout?" he said. "This is for minor bantam."

"I'm thirteen," Rocket said. He pushed the kid's bag to the side and slid his in. "Move over."

"Chill, bro. Wait until I'm done," the kid said.

"Move over and we can talk about it," Rocket said.

He could feel everyone looking at them. This guy was such a jerk.

A kid in a blue pinny moved over.

Rocket sat down. The kid with the curly black hair grunted and moved over as well. Rocket ignored him and began to get dressed as fast as he could. He liked to take his time when he dressed, but he didn't want to sit next to this guy any longer than he had to. Before long, he had his shin pads and pants on and had slipped his feet into his skates. He threw his shoulder and elbow pads on next. He looked into his bag. He had two practice jerseys, one red and one blue, and his Huskies sweaters. Which one should he wear?

The curly haired kid knocked Rocket's leg as he got up.

"You play for anyone last year?" he asked.

He sounded sarcastic, like he expected Rocket to say

house league — so that's what Rocket said.

The kid laughed. "And you're trying out for AAA? You're nuts, bro." He laughed all the way to the door, looked back and then kept laughing as he left.

Rocket reached for his Huskies sweater.

Let's see him laugh when he saw this.

The Doorknobs!

Pathetic.

CHAPTER 7

The players were divided into three groups: red, blue and black. It didn't take Rocket long to figure out the players in black were the returning players. When the coach blew his whistle, after what felt like an endless series of skating drills, all the kids in red and blue raced to centre and dropped to one knee. The kids wearing black continued to fool around, some shooting on the goalie and a few others playing baseball with pucks. The coach didn't seem to care. He was looking at his clipboard. Finally, he blew his whistle again. Only after the third whistle did the kids in black begin to trickle over.

Rocket pressed his stick into the ice to keep calm. Those guys were acting like the tryout was a joke — and it was a joke. Just like the Huskies tryout.

"Nice work. Good effort all around," the coach said. "I want to scrimmage for the last little bit to end the tryout."

That caught Rocket's attention.

"I want lots of passing. You won't impress me by hogging the puck. Even though it's a tryout, I also want to see if you can keep to your positions — and plenty of backchecking. All right?"

"Yeah. Whatever," a few of the boys in black said.

The coach laughed.

This was Rocket's chance. Not much time, but if he put in a solid scrimmage, he'd be a shoo-in.

"To be fair we're going to split up the guys in black," the coach said. "Give me Jeremy's line, with Jonathan and Christopher at the far end. You put on red pinnies. The rest of you will be Blue and play with Aubrey."

Rocket figured Aubrey for a dad. He'd helped with the practice and acted like an assistant coach — which meant he thought he was an awesome player when he wasn't.

"Don't worry about positions," the coach called as the players sorted themselves out. "We'll organize things as we go along."

Another dad-looking type waited for them at the Red bench. "We'll go with the guys in black for the first shift 'cause I know them, and I'll sort out you new guys," he said.

"Wise choice, Dad," Jeremy said, and his teammates laughed.

Rocket hadn't really noticed Jeremy in the drills, except that his mouth was always going.

"With a show of hands, tell me who's a defence-man," Jeremy's dad said.

Three guys put up their hands. Rocket's heart sunk. He could get put on defence.

Duane was next to him. He didn't play with much fire, but maybe he'd been to too many tryouts. Rocket took a chance: "We'll be on a line together," he called out, patting Duane on the back.

Jeremy's dad shrugged. "Yeah, okay. Pick up another winger and you'll be a line." He moved over to organize the rest of the forwards.

"You want to play with us?" Rocket said to the kid next to him. "I'm centre and Duane . . . you're right, I think?" Duane nodded. "You want to go left?" The kid shrugged. "Let's get to the door, so we can go out next."

Rocket filed on the bench and turned to his new left-winger. "What's your name?"

"Patrick."

"Where'd you play last year?"

"I was with the Hawks. It's an A team. I just came to check it out. I'm going back."

"Yeah. That's cool. If you find a team you like . . ." He wasn't too pumped about having a guy like that on his line. Too late now, he figured. "Well, let's see if we can pop a couple in just for fun. I'm always up for a scrimmage."

His linemates didn't respond.

"That's yours, Jeremy!" Jeremy's dad yelled.

Rocket watched as Jeremy raced after a puck deep in the Blue end. He did a spin at the blue line and banged his stick. His dad started laughing.

Aubrey leaned over the partition between the benches. "Jeremy's on fire this year. What're you feeding him?"

"Kid grew three inches, and he's got so much energy, me and Tina are going crazy. If he's not on the ice five times a week he loses it," Jeremy's dad said.

"He's looking good. Keep feeding him whatever you've been cooking 'cause it's working," Aubrey said.

Jeremy's spinning did nothing other than amuse the two dads. The defenceman ringed the puck around the wall to his left-winger. The winger trapped it with his skate, but a bit too casually, because the right defenceman was able to pinch down low and stuff the puck back in. The defenceman and Jeremy fought for possession. The Blue centre and left-winger joined in the scrum. Then another defenceman crept over. Rocket counted five guys in the corner.

"Case of the bunchies, if you ask me," Rocket said to his linemates. "Half the guys on the ice are there. If we spread out we'll definitely get some goals."

Patrick didn't answer. Duane nodded and took a sip of water.

The puck squirted free behind the net and the Blue defenceman sent it around the other way. Virtually the same thing happened: the pinch, the puck in the corner and a scrum.

"These guys are like fish in a bowl," Rocket said. "They chase everything. Keep wide when we're in possession and converge on the net when someone has a good shot." He looked at the clock. "If they ever get off. We'll barely get a couple of shifts."

Duane took another sip of water. "Good. I can rest up for my next tryout," he said.

Rocket was beginning to regret his linemate choices. These guys couldn't care less. He looked up at Jeremy's dad. Jeremy had been on for two minutes. The play drifted from end to end. The boys were treating the scrimmage more like shinny. Guys only skated when they had the puck, so no one got tired.

Rocket banged the boards with his stick. "Long shift, Jeremy. Change it up."

A defenceman had the puck two metres inside the Blue zone. Jeremy lunged at it, but the defenceman passed it to his partner. Jeremy continued forward and jumped on the defenceman's back and the two boys fell to the ice. The defenceman gave Jeremy a face wash with his glove, and then rolled over and got to his feet. Jeremy tried to trip him with his stick, but he hopped to his right and got away. Jeremy stayed on his back for a while and then slowly — painfully slow for Rocket — rose to his knees and, finally, one skate at a time, to his feet. Rocket banged the boards again with his stick.

"Get off, already. Come on," Rocket yelled.

Jeremy paid no attention. He skated back to the Red end to join the play.

"Okay, Jeremy, let's change it up. Let's go," his dad yelled.

Jeremy obviously didn't care what his dad said, because he ignored him completely and instead began to tackle guys. Soon everyone was fooling around. Two guys even pretended to fight. The whistle blew.

"Finally," Rocket fumed.

"Good fun," the coach said. "Give me three hard laps around the ice to end it off." He blew his whistle again.

Rocket stared in disbelief. The scrimmage was over? He smacked the top of the boards with his glove. "That was ridiculous! Can you believe it?" he said to Duane.

"I'm not doing three more laps. I'm going to the dressing room," Duane said. He took his extra stick and headed to the door.

Rocket stepped out on the ice. In a few quick strides, he was at top speed. He needed to show them why they called him the Rocket. This was his last chance. Spurred by his anger, he zipped past the other players. Jeremy had no respect for the game — a seven-minute shift! Mr. Big Shot, because his dad was assistant coach.

"Look at that little guy go," he heard someone say. Rocket looked over his shoulder. It was the curly haired guy from the dressing room. A shoulder in the rib cage would shut him up quick. But he couldn't. He needed to make this team and show Barker he'd made a huge mistake. Rocket finished the three laps first and kept going. Too much pent-up energy and frustration: he needed to skate. He carved on the inside edges of his skates, curling behind the net, a crisp scrape sounding with each stride, the wind in his face, nothing but open ice in front of him.

A whistle blew.

"You, number 164. Off the ice! Zamboni is waiting." The coach banged his stick on the boards.

Rocket dragged his right skate to slow down. "Sorry, I lost track of laps and . . ."

"Okay. Let's get changed. Thanks for coming out," the coach said.

His tone worried Rocket. "My name's Bryan Rockwood. I played for the Huskies last year."

The coach gave him an awkward smile. "I probably have all your information. Thanks for coming out and good luck."

He didn't have a clue who he was! "I played AAA last year — for the Huskies," he said desperately.

The coach nodded a few times. "I'll . . . um . . . I

have to meet with some parents now. If you want I can speak with your parents later, but you'll have to wait half an hour or more because there's lots of paperwork and stuff. So let's get changed."

Rocket stared at him. This wasn't possible. The Doorknobs weren't going to sign him? His line probably scored more goals last year than their entire team put together. He left the ice and walked to the dressing room, his mind spinning, almost feeling sick to his stomach. Again, he was the last guy in. It was crowded.

He was too angry to be polite. He marched to his spot.

"For the last time, move over!" he snarled.

The curly haired boy rolled his eyes. "Chill out, little guy. You going to have a temper tantrum?"

"No. I'm going to plow your face through the boards when we play you," Rocket said.

He laughed. "Not sure what dream world you're living in. 'We' aren't going to play. This is AAA, bro, not house league."

"You're such an idiot,". Rocket scoffed. "Look at this sweater. Recognize it?"

"Yeah. The Huskies. So?"

"So I played on the Huskies last year, AAA, and we sort of won the championship, and I sort of won the scoring title."

Rocket knew he sounded arrogant, but this was ridiculous. They weren't going to sign him?

"Why aren't you playing with them again?"

"Not your problem," Rocket said. "Worry about your own game."

"I should've gone to the other room," he said. "And you need to chill, bro."

"You can sit here," Duane piped up.

He was sitting on the other side of the room and had made some space.

Rocket grabbed his bag and clothes and gave the curly haired boy a harsh look.

"Thanks. Guy's a jerk," he said to Duane. "Thinks he's a big shot 'cause he plays on the Doorknobs."

The door opened and Duane's dad came in. He looked like he'd won the lottery. "Duaner! You were awesome out there, especially on those one-on-ones. That's what I'm talking about." He leaned forward and whispered, "We just got an offer. How awesome is that? You made it. I'm so stoked, I can't believe it! Coach is an awesome guy. I really like him. I talked to Aubrey, too. Strong coaching staff. I offered to coach, but they're set, so I'm going to be an assistant manager keeping the stats."

Duane said something in his dad's ear. His dad looked over at Rocket, shrugged and whispered something back. His phone rang and he frowned. "It's the Aces. The manager keeps bugging me for an answer. May as well get this over with." He pressed a button. "Hey, man. Good to hear from you. Sorry, I'm in a rink and the reception's bad. Didn't get your call." He walked out.

Duane rubbed his knees with his hands. "You should've made it," he said to Rocket quietly. "I asked my dad. He said they thought you were too small. I figured you'd want to know."

Rocket couldn't find the words. A week ago, he

would've laughed in someone's face if they'd said he couldn't make the Wilmont Demons.

"To be honest, I don't want to play for them, either," Duane said. He actually looked upset. "I had friends on my last team. I don't know anyone here. And I'm sick of never having time for anything else. I'd quit, but my dad would freak out. He thinks I'm going to the NHL. He even tells people that."

He looked so sad Rocket had to feel sorry for him.

Duane raised his eyebrows. "I'll give you my size if you give me your speed."

Rocket had to laugh. "Deal."

"So who else have you tried out for?" Duane said.

"No one, yet. I'll find something. I'm not worried."

Duane's mouth twisted into a half-smile. "My dad's been going crazy because he says all the teams are filled up. You might want to hurry and make a decision."

"Yeah. My mom's on top of it. I'll be okay."

A sick feeling rolled over him. How would he be okay? Wilmont was one of the worst teams in AAA, and they'd cut him.

Could it really be over?

Was this the end of the line?

CHAPTER 8

Rocket slid the chocolate powder across the table. Maddy tossed a couple of spoonfuls into her mug and stirred, the spoon clinking against the sides. She kept stirring and stirring.

"Bugging you yet?" She grinned.

"In about a minute I'm going to throw myself over the balcony, but otherwise not really," Rocket said.

"I figured you couldn't take it. You're soft, Rockwood."

He patted his stomach. "I did three hundred sit-ups this morning. Check it out."

She pointed to his head. "I meant there."

He pushed the cookies toward her. "Eat up, chubby." It was an old joke of theirs. Maddy was rail thin.

Maddy pretended to pout. "I brought them to cheer you up, and I've eaten them all and you haven't had one."

"I'm in training."

"One cookie is going to make you fat?"

"I . . . Maybe later."

She groaned and took another bite of cookie. "Bryan, you have to lighten up."

"It's not that. I'm not hungry."

She took a tiny bite and nodded slowly. "You didn't tell me about your tryout last night with the Demons. That's a serious name, by the way. What do their sweaters look like? Do they have a one-eyed monster holding a stick?"

"Sort of. More like a green-faced little guy with mad hair. Anyway, the tryout was a waste. Totally lame team. We barely did any drills, and this idiot stayed on the ice for ten minutes when we scrimmaged and I didn't get to play. Team has no discipline. No way am I playing for them; I'm not that desperate. I don't want to lose every game this year, either, thanks very much."

Maddy put her cookie down. "So when's the next tryout?"

It had been two days since the Wilmont tryout, and the sting of getting cut was still painful.

"Don't know."

"But you told me teams get filled up . . . like there are basically no spots after a few days."

"Um . . . Yeah. I guess."

"What are you going to do?"

"I'll figure it out."

"But why didn't you just play for Wilmont so you at least have a team?" she said.

His stomach dropped. For some stupid reason he could never lie to her. Sometimes it was irritating.

"I . . . I got cut again," he said.

She stared at him, clearly in shock. "But you told me they weren't any good? How did that happen? You played on the best team, and now you can't make one of the worst? Are there any other teams?"

"Not in AAA, and I can't drop a level. Once you do, it's impossible to go back up. You get labelled."

She gave him a sad smile.

"It's not that bad," he said. "Seriously. Lots of guys move around between now and September when the season starts. Guys accept offers and then get a better one and leave an opening. I heard of a guy last year who signed in September with the Kings."

"Are the Kings any good?"

"Good? They played us in the finals. I think the smart thing is to play it cool and wait. Something will open up, for sure."

Maddy popped the rest of her cookie into her mouth and chewed slowly. "So your strategy is to do nothing until September?" She didn't sound impressed.

"I'm not saying that. I'll definitely keep looking. But tryouts are basically done for AAA. No point panicking."

"I thought it was 'bring it?'"

"I'll 'bring it' when I play against the Huskies and get a hat trick."

"Mr. Rockwood, you really are the most serious boy I've ever met. You may know hockey, but I know something you don't."

"That's very unlikely," he said, "but go ahead."

"This situation calls for a cheer-me-up chocolate bar. Fortunately, someone you admire very much — someone you worship, to be more precise — got paid yesterday for delivering newspapers." She pulled out a ten-dollar bill.

He patted his stomach again. "Thanks. This is a chocolate-free zone."

"Oh, come on. Don't be so boring. Are we going to sit here all night and talk about AAA and hockey and Wilmont and Huskies? Let's go before it gets too late."

"I can't slack off now," Rocket said. He wanted her to understand how important this was. He couldn't blow his hockey career by stuffing his face with junk food. "It took me time to figure it out, but I think I get why the Huskies cut me. I'd lost my intensity. I was always joking around in the locker room and on the ice. I was overconfident and I thought I could just walk on and make the team. I can't do that at my size. I've learned my lesson, big time. I have to earn it, every practice, every shift, every game."

"You're thirteen, Bryan."

"You don't understand what it takes to make it," he said.

She was just like everyone else.

"Make it? How many guys make it to the NHL — one in a thousand, in ten thousand, in a hundred thousand?" she said.

"You mean how many guys *my size* make it?" he thundered.

Maddy's eyes softened. "That's not what I meant. Okay, Mr. Serious, I got another idea. Why don't I buy two chocolate bars and I'll eat mine and you can watch me eat yours."

Rocket relaxed his shoulders and rested his hands on the table. "I'll have one bite to make you feel better."

She pouted. "Do you have to?"

The front door opened.

"Hi, Risa," Maddy called out. "How's it going?"

His mom came into the kitchen. "I'm doing well. How are you both?"

"Awesome," Maddy said. "How was work?"

"Exhausting, as usual." His mom paused. "Hi, Bryan."

"Hi," he murmured.

His mom smiled. "I have some interesting news to cheer up Mr. Grumpy-Pants," she said.

"I like that even better than Mr. Serious," said Maddy. "Suits him."

Rocket closed his eyes for a moment to let his irritation pass.

"I won't keep you in suspense," his mom said. "It's obviously too much for you. Greg texted me. He found a team."

Rocket sat up.

"Look at that. All interested in your mommy now, aren't you?"

"I'm just tired, Mom. And you made me grumpy by calling me grumpy."

"Gee. Sorry, Bryan."

"I accept your apology."

She looked at her phone. "The team is called the Bowmont Blues and they're having a tryout in a couple of days — Friday, I think. Greg spoke to the coach, and she said she'd love for you to come out." His mom looked at him and wrinkled her brow. "What's wrong now?" she asked.

"Does it have to do with the fact the coach is a she?" Maddy said.

"Please," his mom said. "You haven't even met her."

As usual, they didn't get it. He could care less if the coach was a she, a he or an *it*. "Bowmont's not in AAA," he said.

"Is that really so important?" his mom said. "I'm sure it's a good team, or Greg wouldn't have recommended it." She looked back at her phone. "It's a AA team."

Rocket reached for the laptop and typed in the name. The Bowmont Blues, AA: tenth place. He felt like his blood was draining from his body. He searched for the standings from last season.

"Bryan? What's up?" Maddy said.

He felt like throwing up.

"Bryan?" his mom said softly.

He spun the laptop around for them to see. "Last place," he said. "Last place — zero wins." He waited for it to sink in

"Bryan, it's going to be okay," his mom said. "If this works out, and from the sound of it the coach is very interested, then you have a team. That's the point, isn't it?"

If Maddy hadn't been there, he might have lost it. Bowmont was the worst team in AA — which meant they weren't really a AA team, not with zero wins. Was he that desperate? What if Ty or Adam heard? He'd be the joke of the school. The put-downs would be brutal.

Maddy caught his eye. "Didn't you say spots open up all the time?"

"I might've exaggerated about that a bit," he said, too miserable to pretend otherwise.

"Then you'll play for Bowmont and prove them all wrong," Maddy said.

"I . . . I don't know. Scouts don't watch AA games. I have to think about it. Maybe I'm done . . . Maybe." He stood up. "Sorry. I'm tired. I'll take a pass on the chocolate bars, Maddy. Thanks. I think I'll go to bed. Tell Ty's dad I'm not sure. Tell him thanks, too. I just have to . . ."

He left the kitchen before they could see his face.

CHAPTER 9

He ran through the puddle. The water splashed his ankles and made his saggy track pants a little heavier. Rocket wiped his eyes with his sleeve, jumped down off the curb and crossed the road to the park.

Other than the occasional delivery truck and the odd early riser, the streets were deserted. Although at six in the morning he didn't expect much action. The path around the park was muddy from the rain, so he shifted over and ran through the trees. The sloshing sound as his feet slogged through the soft turf was comforting; it was almost like having a running buddy. Three laps and he'd be done. He found it a struggle to breathe in the damp, cool air. He needed to push through it, though.

Had his fitness been the difference at the Huskies tryout? When you were his size, you needed to be the fittest guy on the ice.

Rocket slipped between two evergreen trees. Water from the branches fell onto him. This was no fun. He saw his apartment building and longed to go back and slide into bed for another hour before he had to get up for school. Instead, he put his head down and rounded the corner. He'd promised himself he'd run to the library and back, then do three laps in the park, so that's what he was going to do. He trudged along and finished his second lap. That cheered his spirits and he picked up the pace, pretending it was late in the third period and it was up to him to win it for the Huskies.

He checked himself. The Huskies weren't his team anymore.

"Hey, Marathon Man. You're wet. Trust me."

He waved at Maddy and held up his finger to show her he had one more lap. Then he began sprinting full out.

At the end, he blasted between the evergreens, slid on two feet and stopped in front of Maddy, throwing in some jazz hands.

"If hockey doesn't work out you can always fall back on your mud-boy dancing act," she said.

"It's more a hobby than a passion," he said, his hands falling to his sides. He was tired.

"You in the NHL yet?"

"Soon," he said.

They walked back to the building. He liked running early, before all the cars and people showed up and things got noisy. Somehow the streets and buildings weren't so ugly and grey in the morning.

"I forgot to tell you," he said. "I got some major news—"

"I heard already," Maddy interrupted. "You memorized your phone number. You're such a clever boy, aren't you?"

"I forgive you for being sarcastic, because I know you're only covering up your insecurities." He grinned and gave her a little shove.

She held her arms out. "And the news is?"

"Guess."

"Bryan, you're so lame."

"C'mon. Guess. I'll give you a clue. It's about Grady." Maddy looked surprised.

He waited.

Her eyes narrowed.

"Okay, fine. I'll tell you," he said. "I did a search on Grady's name. He told me he'd played for Springfield, which used to be a famous hockey team in the American Hockey League. And he did! There was a Grady Graham who played for Springfield about twenty-three years ago. He didn't play for Eddie Shore, but he really did play professional hockey."

"Get out of here!" Maddy shrieked. "No way it's him — and who's Eddie Shore?"

"Tsk, tsk. How can you not know Hall-of-Famer Eddie Shore? The Bruins retired his number. He played from the 1920s to the 1940s, and then he bought the Springfield Indians and coached for years. He was dead before Grady played."

"How do you know it was our Grady?"

"I saw the team picture. I can't believe how much he's changed, but you can still tell. They called him the G-Man, I guess because of his initials. He was pretty good, too. Got lots of penalty minutes, but in his last year he scored twenty-seven goals, which isn't bad for a tough guy."

"What happened to him?"

"I read an article from back then that said he got hurt. I guess old Grady was telling the truth when he said he'd wrecked his knee." Rocket kicked a pop can to her.

She dribbled it a couple of steps and kicked it back. "Weird story."

"It is," Rocket agreed. He kicked the can ahead. "So, you coming over tonight?"

She eyed him closely, then sighed. "You've forgotten already."

"Huh?"

"The tryout? Griffen's all freaked out because your mom's borrowing his precious car."

Rocket crunched the can. "I haven't decided to go."

"Because?"

He shrugged.

Grady was sitting by the doors, slumped against the wall, his head bobbing up and down.

"Yo, Grady, I read about your hockey career at Springfield. Major props," Rocket said.

Grady groaned and buried his head into his chest.

"Grady?" Rocket said.

Maddy pulled on his arm and pressed her finger to her lips. They walked past him and into the lobby.

"That's about the worst I've seen him," Rocket said.

"It's that new bar that's opened around the corner, The Grove. Guys go out back to the laneway to smoke, and Grady gets drinks from them. That place is bad news," she said.

"This neighbourhood is bad news," he said.

"Yeah, well . . . at least it's ours." She pushed the

elevator button. "Thanks for helping me deliver my papers, by the way."

"Seriously? I have to stretch, do my push-ups and sit-ups, and then get ready for school."

She rolled her eyes. "Really?"

"The Huskies did me a favour; it was a wake-up call. I'm going to get stronger, go harder on the puck, fill the net with pucks and show them they made a mistake. I'll make them take me back."

"Why play for them after what they did?"

The elevator opened. They stepped in, and she hit the button for the second floor.

"The Huskies are the best." Rocket shrugged. "Scouts look at the players on the best teams. It's as simple as that."

"But . . . since you can't play for the Huskies, who are you going to play for?"

"I . . . That's the part of the plan I haven't figured out."

"Then?"

"I don't know!" he yelled, and kicked the elevator door with the side of his foot. "Everyone keeps asking me who I'm going to play for. What am I supposed to say? That all the AAA teams stiffed me and that I'm trying out for some lame AA club called Bowmont? The rest of this year, and next, is going to be a nightmare."

"Hockey players are hard to take sometimes," Maddy said. The doors opened and they walked out. A pile of newspapers was stacked on a trolley.

"What does that mean?"

"There are some AAA guys at my school; they're all

puffed up and they wear their jackets all the time. They act like they're in the NHL already," she said.

"So I'm puffed up?" Rocket felt himself getting mad. Of course guys wore their hockey jackets to school. He did.

"You put other guys down all the time if they're not playing AAA or if they're not on the Huskies — like how good people are at hockey is the only thing that matters. How do you know what Bowmont's going to be like? Maybe they're going to be better this year. You haven't even seen them play — and you haven't made the team, by the way."

"Is this you cheering me up?"

"This is me telling you to stop whining about the stupid Huskies and get on a team and play already or I'm going to kill you." She was red in the face and her fists were clenched. For a second he thought she was actually going to hit him.

They stood looking at each other. Rocket wanted so badly to yell something back, to tell her that she didn't get it. Except she did get it; she always did. He had been a stuck-up AAA player, but he couldn't be anymore. Not if he wanted to play hockey.

Maddy's fists slowly unclenched. "I know you're mad and embarrassed and seriously pissed. But aren't you the guy who told me the game is won by the team that wants it the most? This is your third period. If you really want to make it, so what if a bunch of puffed up AAAers at your school start making fun of you? Forget them. Does the Rocket quit that easily?"

He shook his head. Then he reached for one of the papers.

"I want you to know that I'm only going to help you deliver your stupid papers because you're too useless to do it yourself," he said. "Also, you can't kill me — I'm your only friend. And, just for you, I'll go to the stupid tryout." He grinned and looked down at the paper in his hand. "Do people still read these? Why don't they download them like normal people?"

"You got doors 201, 202, 207, 208, 211 and 214."

"You can count on me."

"I know I can." She said it very seriously.

Rocket began to put the papers in front of the doors.

"I forgot to ask. What did Ty and Adam do when you got cut?" she called out.

He threw a paper in front of apartment 214. "Nothing. What could they do?"

"Speak to the coach. Get you back on the team. Do *something*? Aren't they your best friends?"

"Yeah. But it doesn't work that way."

Maddy pulled the trolley to the elevator and pressed the button. The doors opened right away and she pushed it in. They rose to the third floor. "Thanks for helping," she said, "and you got 301, 302, 303 and 306." The doors opened. "Now get to work."

Rocket went to the end of the hall. He'd been struggling over the decision to go to the Bowmont tryout for two days, and she got him to agree to go in two minutes! She was wrong about school, though. It wasn't going to be easy to ignore what the guys would say — not when he'd been known as the Rocket: the big shot hockey player with the Huskies jacket. When they found out he was playing for the worst team in

67

AA, that whole image was going to backfire on him.

"Hurry up. Papers don't deliver themselves — and there's a Crunchie bar in it for you," Maddy said.

"Can't do a Crunchie. Got a tryout tonight," Rocket said.

CHAPTER 10

Rocket shuffled his books and papers into a stack and stuffed them into the bottom of his locker. Grade six had been so much easier — one teacher, one room. Now they had to move from class to class. He kept forgetting things and having to run to his locker after every period. All around him, kids tossed their books into their lockers and grabbed their lunch bags.

The idea of lunch brought a smile to his face. One thing wasn't going to change this year: the Butt Kickers were going to win intramural floor hockey.

He and Ty had formed the team in grade four and ended up beating a grade five team for the championship. They hadn't lost a game since, and with Ty, Adam and him on the floor, they'd won the championship again last year. Adam had posted on Facebook that he'd recruited two more AAA players, Brandon Harrison and Nicolas Kingstone. Rocket barely knew them. They'd just come to Forest Mills for grade seven. Adam had started hanging out with them after Christmas. Rocket had written back that he didn't think they needed more guys, but Ty didn't seem to care.

Rocket grabbed his lunch. It would be a squat and gobble: the Butt Kickers' first game was in fifteen minutes. His locker door slammed shut, and he spun around. Adam and Ty were laughing.

"Did we scare you?" Adam said.

"Only now that I see your faces," Rocket said.

"Let's scare each other in the caf," Ty said. "The guys are meeting us there, and I want time to eat."

Adam elbowed Rocket. "Guys, check this out." He grinned and nodded across the hall at a boy opening his locker.

"Hey, Big Red," Adam said, "I can't remember the capital of Venezuela."

The boy stuffed his books into his locker. "Look it up — it's called the internet," he said, without turning around.

"Oh, c'mon," Adam said, a huge smile on his face. "I don't have my phone with me and it's been bugging me all day. You're on the Forest Mills trivia team. You must know it. You know everything about stuff that's not important."

The boy closed his locker and set off down the hall.

"Big Red, this isn't you. We're bros. Dude? It's me. Ad-man! Call me and we'll hang!"

Big Red turned the corner, and Adam and Ty burst out laughing. Rocket smiled, but he wished his friend would leave people alone. A few years ago, Adam had come up with the nickname Big Red — because of the kid's curly red hair. He'd made the guy's life miserable ever since.

"He kills me," Adam said. "Is he not the funniest guy ever?"

They went down the stairs and headed to the cafeteria. A few kids were milling around the door. Rocket barrelled right through; when you were on the Butt Kickers, you didn't wait for people to get out of the way. He spotted the other guys on the team sitting at their usual table by the window. He remembered when he came to Forest Mills and had to eat with the big kids. He'd been terrified. That's when he'd met Ty and Adam, huddled by the little tables at the front, the worst ones. Sure enough, the grade fours were sitting there.

All the boys at his table were wearing hoodies with their hockey team's logo. Rocket had thrown his Huskies hoodie under his bed. He felt a little self-conscious being the only kid without one, and tried to look casual and relaxed. This is no big deal, he told himself.

"Yo, Butt Kickers. We stoked for the annual championship run?" Rocket said.

"We got it in the bag with Harry and Kinger," Adam said.

Adam held out a fist and the two boys punched it. For a second Rocket was confused, but then he got it. Harry was Brandon Harrison and Kinger was Nicolas Kingstone. Harry and Kinger both wore Rangers jackets.

"Can you move over a bit?" Rocket asked Kinger. The table was crowded.

Kinger took a bite from his sandwich and pointed with his elbow to the next table. "Sit there, bro," he mumbled.

"Um . . . What did you . . . What?" Rocket said.

Kinger made a big show of gulping his food. "Sit over there, bro. No room."

Rocket took a step forward.

"He's just messing with you," Ty broke in. He laughed, although it sounded hollow to Rocket. "Move over, Kinger."

Kinger grimaced and shifted over a bit. Rocket was about to say something, but decided to let it go and get to lunch. They had to play soon. The guy was obviously a jerk. Since when did Adam have the right to add guys on his own, anyway?

"Hey, Ad-man, did I tell you we're going to Boston and Michigan for tourneys next season?" Kinger said.

"Going to be wicked trips," Harry said.

"Nice try," Adam said. "Huskies are off to Europe. That's called an In Your Face Disgrace, in case you're keeping score." He and Ty high-fived.

Kinger shrugged. "I'll give you that one. We're focused on the season more than tourneys, anyway. This year is going to be different. You watch. Rangers will totally surprise."

"You'll surprise by making the playoffs, bro," Adam said. "Huskies smoked you last season, and we'll smoke you worse this year. We're stacked, bro. You won't even see it coming."

Ty and the other guys were laughing. Rocket didn't see what was so funny. Sounded more like bragging.

"Whatever," Kinger said. "We loaded up, too. We picked up that number nine from the Red Wings. That dude is awesome."

"I remember him," Ty said. "He's a centre, right?"

Kinger and Harry nodded. Rocket remembered, too. He'd gone head-to-head with him in the semi-finals practically every shift — and he'd outscored him.

Kinger tilted his head slightly toward Rocket, and with a half-smile said, "So where are you playing?"

Definitely not the question Rocket wanted to answer in front of this crew. "Not sure. Got a few more tryouts."

"Ty told me his dad set you up with the Demons," Adam said.

Rocket shot Ty a look. He'd told him to keep that quiet. Ty looked down at the table.

"Wilmont! C'mon. They're, like, the saddest team in the world," Harry said. "You can't play for them."

"They're not that bad," Ty said.

"Remember when we played them and Coach Neilson told us not to score after the first period?" Adam said. "I had three open nets, but I had to shoot wide on purpose."

"Remember that game against the Blackhawks when you got benched?" Harry said to Kinger.

"It's 6–0 after one period," Kinger said, grinning. "Coach tells us to lay off. I say, 'Hockey is hockey, and you play at one speed — all out.' I went end-to-end and roofed one, and he sat me for the rest of the game."

The guys thought that was funny, too. Rocket was taking a serious dislike to these two guys, especially Kinger.

"What are you going to do?" Adam asked Rocket.

He felt as if a giant spotlight was burning down on him. "Like I said, tryouts aren't over."

"They are for AAA," Harry said. Rocket could tell Kinger was trying not to laugh.

"You don't know everything, bro," Rocket said.

"You should look around more. AA's okay and the

best teams would give most AAA teams a run for it," the kid next to Ty said. He was their goalie, Ben MacDonald. He played for the Young Nationals, or the Nats, as everyone called them, and was possibly the best goalie in AAA.

"My dad told me he'd set up another tryout for you," Ty said. "Who was it with again?"

The spotlight was getting brighter. "I . . . um . . . not sure . . ." Rocket said.

All eyes were on Ty as he looked up to the ceiling, his face fixed in concentration.

"Bowmont," he shouted, and the boys laughed. Ty looked around proudly. "It just popped into my head. Bowmont's the team. You going out for them?"

"Never heard of them," Adam said. "Have you?" he asked Harry.

He shook his head.

"Me, neither," Kinger said. "Are they new?"

"I've heard of them," a kid next to Ty piped up. His name was Thomas Jakobsson. He was Swedish and his dad had actually played on Sweden's national team way back when. Thomas played for the Aeros, a AA team. He'd been on the Butt Kickers since grade four, too. He was a good defenceman.

Rocket put his sandwich down. It tasked like chalk.

"They're AA," Thomas said.

Kinger snickered and covered his face with his hand. Adam looked out the window. The other boys looked uncomfortable.

"We should get going," Ty said. "Game is going to start. Let's go kick some butt."

The boys let out a whoop and together they headed

to the gym. Rocket trailed behind. At least it was out there and he wouldn't have to deal with it again. And if something came up in the next month or so, he'd have the last laugh. Ty opened the gym door to the sound of clashing sticks and pucks ricocheting off the walls. Maybe a little butt-kicking would cheer him up — and, boy, could he use that!

CHAPTER 11

Rocket took a plastic stick from the bin and immediately began to bend the blade to increase the curve. His friends were doing the same. Ty and Adam were talking to Kinger and Harry. After that lunch, he had no desire to join the conversation.

He spotted an orange puck under a bench. He hooked it out with his blade and began to stickhandle rapidly. Ben wasn't ready yet, so when Rocket got close to the net, he wristed the puck up high — too high as it turned out. The puck nicked the crossbar and flipped into the air. Rocket took a few steps closer and swung at it baseball-style. He connected, and the puck flew into the right corner of the net.

Rocket spun, a big grin in place, expecting a cheer from Ty and Adam. They were still talking to Kinger and Harry. He fished the puck out. It was still a chill move, he told himself. Ben grabbed his goalie stick and stepped between the pipes.

"I'll warm you up," Rocket said. He lobbed the puck at Ben's pads. "You guys doing many tournaments?"

"We aren't going to Europe," Ben said.

Rocket laughed and shot again.

"The Huskies are kind of over-the-top that way," Rocket said. "I'm not going to miss that team too much, other than playing with Ty and Adam." He held onto the puck. "Coach is a total jerk, too."

"So you quit?" Ben said, as if surprised.

"Let's say the decision was mutual," Rocket said.

Ben didn't react. Rocket shot a puck to his glove.

"Why aren't you playing for another AAA team?" Ben asked.

Rocket curled the blade of his stick and shot another puck, this time to Ben's blocker. "I think I blew it by waiting too long and I got caught in the numbers game. All the teams have signed guys, but they tell me there will be spots by September. So . . . I guess I wait and see."

Ben slid two pucks back. "Tough, bro. Bit of a risk waiting until September. You could be in house league." He laughed to show he wasn't serious.

"You may be right," Rocket said. "At least I'd get lots of ice time." He fired a low shot.

Ben dropped into a butterfly and kicked it away.

"Ready for a warm-up?" Kinger called out. He shot one from about ten metres out.

Rocket turned around. "What do you think I've been doing?" he snapped.

Kinger ignored him and shot again, a slapper. Ben kicked it out with his left pad. Adam rushed in, banged in the rebound and raised his stick above his head.

"The garbage man is in the house," he said. He curled his blade. "Who we playing, anyway?"

"Don't matter," Kinger growled. He hooked the

puck from Rocket's stick. "I wouldn't try to stop this one. It's going to hurt too much," he said. Ben grunted and got into his stance.

Rocket went over to Ty.

"Why do we need those two guys?" he said quietly. "I mean, for real, do we have to play with Kinger?"

Ty shrugged. "Adam was hyped about it, and he figured if we didn't get them, they'd play for someone else." He paused then added, "And they're AAA."

"Meaning?"

Ty looked away. "Nothing. They're okay guys. Give them a chance."

"What's the okay part of Kinger?"

Ty didn't answer.

"It's our team, yours and mine," Rocket said. "Adam shouldn't decide things like this — at least not by himself."

"It's no big deal, just intramurals."

He obviously wasn't interested. Rocket changed the topic. "You want to do something this Saturday? Take shots on the wall?"

He and Ty often spent hours firing tennis balls at targets on the school wall.

"I got practice, then I think Money's dad is having lunch for us at his golf club. Maybe after."

Rocket nodded glumly.

A whistle blew. A kid wearing a referee's jersey stood in the middle of the gym and waved his hand. "Sorry I'm late. Let's get going."

Ty bounced his blade on the floor a few times. "So . . . let's get some more hardware for the Butt Kickers."

That was more like Ty. "Sounds good," Rocket said. "We need to graduate next year with a perfect record."

"Bring it," Ty said.

"Bring it," Rocket repeated.

Adam, Kinger and Harry came over.

"We got too many men," Rocket said. "Only four at a time."

"Solve the problem," Kinger said.

Harry snickered.

Rocket and Kinger locked eyes. "I started this team in grade four," Rocket said. "Me and Ty. Maybe the newest guys on the team should solve the problem."

"C'mon, Butt Kickers," the ref said. "I'm dropping the puck."

"AAA players start," Kinger said. "That's only fair. We'll get a lead and then you can come on. We have to make sure we win first."

"You kidding me?" Rocket thundered. "How many goals did you score last season? One?"

"You don't even come up to my knees on the ice. Give me a break."

His mocking tone was even more irritating than his trash talk. Rocket waited for Ty and Adam to say something. They didn't, and their silence was worse than anything Kinger said. He looked each of the four boys squarely in the face.

"You guys are obviously too awesome for me. Good luck with the season and, sorry, but I'm too busy to come to the Butt Kickers' team banquet." To Ty and Adam he added, "And no way I'm good enough for three-on-three, so let's forget that, too."

He dropped his stick and walked away.

"C'mon, Rocket," Ty said. "It's a stupid floor hockey game. You're making a big deal out of nothing."

Rocket kept going. It took all his cool not to lose it. This topped it off. After all the stuff that had happened to him, after getting cut from the Huskies, his best friends do this to him. His life was heading downhill faster than he could have imagined. He pushed the gym doors open and turned down the hall, rage flooding over him in waves. It hurt his chest, even. He was twice the player Kinger was — no, ten times — better than Ty or Adam, too.

He didn't need to play three-on-three. Waste of time.

He didn't want to go to Europe.

He was going way farther than that.

CHAPTER 12

"Hey, Rocket. Hold up."

Ty ran over. He was still holding his floor hockey stick.

"What's that all about, bro? Seriously. It's just floor hockey. You can go on for me. I don't care," Ty said.

A flood of bitterness swept over Rocket. "It's not about that. It's about how stupid it is that Kinger and Harry were invited to the team without asking me . . . or you. Then they decide to start and I'm supposed to sit on the bench like a loser until the great AAA players are finished? It's a joke."

"No one thinks you're a loser. It's just . . . that's always been the rule," Ty said. "AAA players start. I mean, Thomas never complains."

"I am AAA. So what the stupid Huskies cut me because . . ." It hurt too much to say it.

Ty rolled his neck and looked past Rocket down the hall. "I get it. I would be pissed, too, if it happened to me. Maybe next year it will. Who knows? Guys get cut all the time for totally stupid reasons, like the coach doesn't like them, or . . . I don't know. Hockey's weird like that. And, don't get mad, but maybe, like, you're not going to be AAA this year. It's not because you're not a good player, it's just that . . . sometimes things work out like that."

Ty couldn't say it either. It was obvious, though. He thought Rocket was too small for AAA, too.

The door at the end of the hall opened and Adam's head popped out. "Ty. C'mon, bro. We're starting." He didn't look at Rocket. He didn't care.

"I'm coming," Ty said. He looked at Rocket and raised an eyebrow.

"You got a game to play with your AAA friends," Rocket said coldly.

Ty's face grew hard. "Yeah . . . well . . . fine. See you later." He walked back to the gym and disappeared inside.

Rocket stood still, the sound of sticks clashing and shouts for the puck filling the empty hallway. He took a ragged breath, and blinked a few times. He'd never missed a Butt Kickers game in his life. Never.

He headed upstairs. He didn't want to risk someone seeing him like this. Walking over to his locker, he poked his head in it, as if he were looking for something. He almost felt dizzy, like he'd just gotten off a ride at an amusement park. After he grabbed his math books, he closed his locker and sat on the floor.

It was hard to believe what had happened. He'd just walked out on the Butt Kickers, on the three-on-three league, on his two best friends. Over what? Sitting on the bench for two minutes? Rocket shook his head. But he couldn't go back — not with Kinger and Harry playing over him; not with Ty and Adam thinking he didn't deserve to be on the Huskies.

A door opened and some kids came down the hall, first two boys, then two more and a girl behind them. Rocket recognized one of the boys in front — Big Red. This would be awkward. He stared at the floor.

"Woburn's going to be real tough," a boy in a blue shirt said.

"Des, you say that about every team," Big Red said, opening his locker. "We can beat them — we made the quarter-finals last year, and that was without Megan."

"We're still weak in certain areas, like sports. I keep telling you guys that," Des said.

"There aren't that many sports questions, and I've been working on it," Big Red said.

The other kids joined them.

Rocket opened his math textbook and pretended to read. He knew one boy was named Daniel. The girl must be Megan. He vaguely remembered her. She won awards for good marks every year. The other boy was in grade eight. Rocket didn't know his name — but he was probably the tallest kid in school.

"Des is freaked about sports again," Big Red said to them.

"Des is a freak. It's not his fault," the tall kid said.

"Thanks, Bird," Des said.

Bird was a good nickname, Rocket thought. The boy was really skinny and had sharp cheekbones and a thin nose. Adam would give the name a thumbs-up.

"We only have five people, and other teams have six," Des said. He sounded worried. "I'm not trying to be negative, and I know Nigel's trying his best, but you can't know everything and we could use more depth. They ask sports questions."

Nigel! That was Big Red's name. Funny how Rocket had forgotten that.

"Give me a couple more weeks and I'll be better," Nigel said forcefully.

Megan ran her finger over her phone. "Okay, who was the last player in the NHL to play without a helmet?" she said.

"Where'd you get that one?" Bird laughed.

"I searched *Really Obscure Sports Trivia*," Megan said.

They all looked at Nigel.

He bit his lower lip and his eyes flashed angrily.

"Sorry, Nigel," Megan said. "But it proves the point. You're awesome at geography, and you help in all the other categories. We're just weak in sports. Let's be honest."

"So what's the answer?" Daniel said.

Megan laughed. "I didn't check. Hold on." She poked at the screen and then scowled. "This is the flakiest phone in the world. I'm not getting a signal for some reason."

"C'mon," Bird whined like he was a little kid. "I want to know. I *need* to know!"

Rocket laughed to himself. Bird was kind of funny.

They all turned to look at him. He might have laughed a touch too loud.

"Perhaps you'd like to inform us, then?" Megan said, her eyes half-closed.

"Craig MacTavish," Rocket said, sticking out his chin.

Megan looked at him closely, then furiously poked at her phone.

"He's right," Des said, holding his phone up.

"You need a new carrier," Bird said to Megan. "And a phone from this decade."

She rolled her eyes, then looked at Rocket. "How did you know that?"

Rocket shrugged. "I don't know. I'm kind of into hockey, I guess. When the NHL passed a rule that players had to wear helmets, the guys already playing were exempt. MacTavish was the last of those players. He played for Edmonton — and St. Louis and the Rangers." He thought about it. "And maybe Philadelphia, too." But Rocket was sure MacTavish was drafted by someone else. "The Bruins! He was drafted by Boston."

"He's right," Des said, holding up his phone again.

Bird pressed his lips together and crossed his arms, holding his elbows with his hands. "So you're sort of into hockey, are you?"

"I guess," Rocket said.

He wished he'd kept quiet. He didn't know these guys, except for Big Red — Nigel — and he was hardly a friend. Rocket had barely ever talked to the guy. He knew Nigel was pretty smart, though. It was one of the reasons Adam had it in for him; Nigel wouldn't let him copy his tests.

Here with his friends, Nigel seemed like a completely different guy, way more talkative. In class, he almost never said a word. When guys picked on him, he just got really sarcastic.

"I see where this is going," Nigel said. "Bad idea. Let's go. We have ten more minutes to practise."

"Hold on," Daniel said. "So . . . what's your name?"

"That's the one and only *Rocket*," Nigel sneered. "Superstar hockey player."

Megan looked at Nigel out of the corner of her eyes. "You're . . . a Rocket?"

He felt himself flush. "It's like a nickname: my last name's Rockwood."

"Gotcha," Megan said. "Boys are weird."

"Do you like other sports?" Des said.

Rocket figured Des was messing with him.

"I might," he said. "I'm pretty weak on hurling and rhythmic gymnastics, though."

"That's why we have Bird on the team," Megan said.

"Why do you pick on me all the time?" Bird said. "No wonder I have no self-esteem."

Megan tossed her head back and laughed loudly. Rocket had never really noticed her before. She was older, so they'd never been in the same class. She was pretty, though she sure didn't try to be: hair was pulled into a messy ponytail, she didn't wear any makeup and she wore baggy jeans and a sweatshirt. But her skin was striking, smooth and rich, as if it were made of marble, and her eyes were bright blue. She was on the small side — something they had in common. She also seemed like a friendly person, as if she were always on the verge of laughing.

Des looked at his phone again. "Okay, the University of Georgia has a living mascot. What is it and what's its name?"

"It's a dog — Uga. There've been about eight or nine of them," Rocket said. Even when hockey wasn't on, he had the channel on the sports network. He really did know a lot about sports.

"Right, well . . . I'm sold," Bird said. "How would you like to join the most awesome club at Forest Mills?"

"He wouldn't want to join the trivia team, and we don't need him," Nigel said. "Let's go, already."

Nigel was getting seriously hostile. And talk about pathetic. Big Red was dissing the Rocket?

"I got your nickname and last name. You have a first name?" Daniel asked him.

"Bryan works," he said.

"What do you say about joining our team?" Des said. "We meet a few times a week to practise, usually at lunch. You're obviously good at sports trivia, and it just so happens we're a bit weak in that area . . ."

"And you play hockey, right?" Bird said.

"There are always lots of hockey questions," Des said. "You'd be a great help."

"Let me check the waiting list . . ." Bird scanned his phone. "Nope. He's the only one applying so . . ."

"I think it's a good idea," Daniel said.

"I'm all for it," Des said. He looked downright thrilled. Nigel looked anything but.

"Okay by me," Megan said. "First time we've had six players on the team. Come on. I'll fire some more sports questions at you guys."

Rocket got up.

"You do play hockey, right?" Bird said.

Rocket tried not to laugh. "I do — a bit."

"Like, what level?" Bird said.

That was a tricky question right now. "I played AAA last season," Rocket said.

Bird and Daniel looked at each other.

Rocket found the whole thing bizarre. From the

Butt Kickers to the trivia team? He wasn't really going to join, obviously, but he didn't have anything else to do right now and he didn't want to make a big deal of it.

"What American city has three professional sports team that wear the same colour?" Megan said.

CHAPTER 13

The sun dipped behind the gleaming condo, casting a long shadow that covered his building and reached the street. Rocket shivered. He should have worn his Huskies jacket. This one was too thin.

Maddy slid her finger across the screen of her phone and put it in her pocket.

"Griffen says he'll be about ten minutes. Got caught in traffic," she said. "Of course, that probably means he'll be here in twenty…"

Rocket's mom had been forced to take a shift at the last minute; she'd arranged for Griffen to take him.

"What time is it?" he said.

"About two minutes since the last time you asked," she said.

"Very amusing, Madeleine."

She stuck her tongue out at him. "If you were old enough to have a watch or a phone, you'd know it's sixteen minutes after six o'clock."

Rocket squeezed his eyes shut. The tryout started at seven-thirty. They'd be cutting it close. Greg had told his mom that this was Bowmont's third and final tryout and there were only one or two spots left. He couldn't miss it.

Maddy sat on his hockey bag and kicked her feet out.

"This isn't the most comfortable chair I've ever sat on. It is the smelliest, though."

"Then sit somewhere else."

"You got something better?"

Rocket grimaced. He wouldn't want to sit on anything else around here, either. Everything about where they lived was dirty: the apartment building, some of its tenants, Grady. There was an old couch someone had dumped on the side of the driveway. It had been there all winter. Paper and plastic bags littered the front yard.

Rocket was usually too embarrassed to invite friends from school or the Huskies over. They'd think he lived in a slum, which he guessed he sort of did, at least compared to most of them.

That condo tower was so close; he'd seen the fanciest cars going into its parking lot. The two buildings were separated by a parking lot, but they could have been light years apart if you thought about who lived there.

Rocket heard a group of kids coming down the street and his throat went dry.

"This is bad," Maddy said. "We should go inside." Her face was pale and she looked scared.

"We'd look like little kids running away," he said. He backed off a few metres from the sidewalk and turned around as if he was looking at something in the lobby. Maddy came and stood next to him.

"I don't mind looking like a little kid," she whispered.

They were only about ten metres away now. No way

could he grab his hockey bag in time. He held his breath and prayed they'd keep walking. Suddenly, everything got quiet.

"You any good?"

Rocket turned around. Three boys and a girl came toward them, dressed in gang colours. Rocket knew one of them, Connor. He hadn't seen the guy around much lately, but he knew he went to Maddy's school.

"I'm no big deal . . . I play a bit," he answered.

"Hey, I know you," Connor said. "You live here, right?"

Rocket nodded.

"You in peewee or something?" Connor said.

"I play minor bantam," Rocket said.

"Nah, you're in peewee. Little Peewee plays peewee," Connor said.

His friends grinned and elbowed each other, and then they pressed forward, crowding around Connor.

"No. I got it wrong. It's Peepee plays peewee," Connor sneered. He high-fived one of the boys. "Let me show you some tricks. Maybe you can use them in a game." Before Rocket could react, Connor grabbed the two hockey sticks on the ground. "Raja, let me school ya in the game of hockey," he said, tossing a stick over.

Rocket winced as the blade bounced off the sidewalk.

Connor reared back and swung at a pop can half-buried in the grass. The can popped up. He chopped at it again. This time it flew in the air and onto the road. "Get down there and I'll show you how it's really done."

Raja grinned and ran down the street a bit. Rocket

noticed he had *Brigade* written in marker on the back of his jacket. He'd never heard of that gang.

Connor began to stickhandle the pop can toward Raja. He'd obviously never played, because he held the stick all wrong, with both hands near the butt. When he was a couple of metres away, he pushed the can past Raja, lowered his shoulder and plowed into him. Raja fell to the road, Connor laughing all the while. He stood over him. He had *Brigade* on his jacket, too.

"Want to go? Want to drop the gloves? Huh? C'mon."

Raja was smiling, but Rocket could see he was hurt — and scared. Raja rolled away.

"I got a better idea," Raja said. He leapt to his feet and ran to Rocket's hockey bag. He winked at his friends, opened the bag, threw the hockey pants aside, and pulled out the shoulder pads. He put them on, even though they were ridiculously small on him. "Now I'm ready to play." He struck a bodybuilder pose.

"Awesome look, Raja," Connor said.

Rocket felt sick. He had to do something. "I got a tryout soon . . . so can I sort of have my stuff back?" he said.

Connor stared at him open-mouthed. "Did you . . . Did I hear that Peewee wants his stuff back?"

Rocket swallowed painfully. "It's no big deal; just have to get going so . . ."

Connor put the point of the blade on the road and rested his hands on the butt-end. "So you'll be needing this, I guess, to score goals and generally be a peewee superstar?"

Rocket's chest pounded.

"There's one problem, though," Connor said. He took the stick with both hands and smashed it on the road. Nothing happened. Connor stared at it for a second and his face darkened; then he smashed it again. His friends began giggling.

"Stupid stick is made of metal," Connor said. He turned the blade around and smashed the stick tip first. His friends were doubled over laughing, because the stick wouldn't break. He let out a roar and took an extra-hard swing. Then Connor held the stick up proudly. The blade dangled from the shaft, held only by the tape.

"I should finish the job," he said, and he kicked at the shaft: three, four, five, then six times. Beads of sweat appeared on his forehead and he began to breathe heavily. Rocket felt an incredible sadness. Those sticks cost over two hundred dollars. Money's dad had bought them for the team. No chance his mom could afford another.

"Let me do it," Raja said, tossing his stick aside. He flexed his arms, slapped Rocket's shoulder pads and let out a warrior call.

Connor's eyes were blazing. "Forget the stupid stick. He can have it back." He swung it over his head and heaved it toward the building. It bounced a couple of times on the pavement and landed off to the side. He looked over at the second stick. "I'm feeling it now. Give me that one," he said to Raja.

Maddy pushed past Rocket and snatched the stick.

"W-what the . . . ?" Connor stuttered.

Maddy raced into the building. Rocket's knees felt weak as the Brigade crew turned to him.

"Peepee's girlfriend saved his stick," Connor said. "What's she going to do about this?" He took the hockey bag by the straps, spun himself around two times to gather speed and then flung the bag across the street.

A police car turned the corner and came toward them.

Connor glared at him. "We'll see you around, Peepee." He started walking away. "C'mon, guys. We'll cut through the back."

They ran off toward the back of the building chanting, "Peepee plays peewee," over and over.

"Could you at least give me my shoulder pads?" Rocket called after them. They disappeared from view.

The police car stopped and the window rolled down. "Is everything all right?" an officer asked. "We got a call about a disturbance."

"Everything's good," Rocket said.

He knew better than to squeal on Connor and his crew.

The cop looked doubtful. "You sure?"

Rocket nodded.

He looked at Rocket for a second. "Okay, we'll do another drive around to make sure."

The window rolled up and he drove off.

Rocket closed his eyes and took a deep breath. For a second he wished he could make himself live somewhere else; he did that a lot when he was younger, like when his parents separated. Like then, nothing changed when he opened his eyes. He still lived in a crappy building, surrounded by garbage and gangs.

He crossed the street. One glove had popped out of his bag, but the rest of the stuff had stayed in. He checked his skates. Fortunately, the blades hadn't hit the pavement. He zipped the bag up and carried it back. Then he remembered. Maddy!

Grady staggered out from around the corner of the building, holding Rocket's broken stick. "Hey, Bryan. I got me a hockey stick." He grinned wildly. "You wanna play me? I used to be good, real good. I played in . . . I was in . . . I was real good." He burped loudly. His breath reeked.

"Not now, Grady," Rocket said, brushing by him and into the lobby.

Maddy stood against the wall, holding his stick in two hands like a club. Her face was pale and it looked like she'd been crying.

"You okay?" she said.

"I'm okay. They didn't do much, just beat up my equipment a bit and stole my shoulder pads. A cop car came by and they ran off. I got lucky."

"I hate them. That girl, Tina, was even my friend in grade four. She was normal up until last year when she started hanging with that crew. They call themselves the Brigade and act all tough and bully kids. They're such bad news. One day, I'm going to . . ." She shook the stick in the air.

"First thing is, you need to give me that stick," Rocket said, grinning.

Maddy blushed and gave it to him. "I might've gotten carried away there," she said.

"Second," he said, "you're one crazy, cool lady to grab my stick like that. You didn't call the cops, too, did you? How did they get here so fast?".

"I called 9-1-1 while everyone was watching

Connor hit that stupid can," she said. "I had to do something, otherwise you couldn't try out tonight."

"I still can't. I don't have shoulder pads. That Raja idiot stole them."

"You're playing. I risked my life for your hockey career. Can't you use a couple of sweatshirts or something?"

"How lame is that?"

"Hey, you've told me that tryouts don't have much contact."

"I'll look stupid."

"A couple of sweatshirts and towels, or . . . I don't know. But hurry up. Griffen will be here soon. Find *something* to use."

"Maddy, I'm not going."

She stomped her foot. "All you ever talk about is hockey, hockey, hockey, and now you're going to quit because some idiot stole your shoulder pads? Some hockey player you are."

"Like you know."

"Quitter."

"Forget you."

"Peepee's a quitter."

Rocket wanted to smash his stick to bits — until he noticed the corners of her mouth rising ever so slightly. His shoulders slumped and he leaned his chin on the butt of his stick.

"Why do I bother hanging out with you?"

"Because I'm a crazy, cool lady."

"That must be it."

She pressed the elevator button. "Get creative. Make that stupid team. And don't break that stick."

The door opened. Rocket gritted his teeth and headed in. He looked back. "Thanks, Maddy," he said.

"Hurry up," she said.

Grady pushed the door open with the shaft of Rocket's broken stick. "Hey, Maddy. You got a quarter for me?"

"You okay with him?" Rocket said.

Maddy rolled her eyes. "If I can handle Connor and his crew, I think I can deal with Grady."

Rocket held the doors for a moment. "What about Connor? You're on his radar now."

She rolled her eyes again. "He's not as tough as he talks. I can deal with his type. Now hurry up. Go!"

Rocket let the doors close.

Towels for shoulder pads?

This was even more pathetic than the trivia team.

CHAPTER 14

Rocket let out a loud sigh of relief as the last player left the dressing room. The only good thing about being late for the tryout was that he could put on his shoulder pads without anyone seeing him.

On the drive over, he and Maddy had made them out of a sweatshirt, towels and duct tape. Griffen had been his usual jerky self and asked if they wanted to use his chewing gum for elbow pads. It was sort of funny the first time, but in typical Griffen style, he'd repeated it about five more times. How did Maddy put up with him? How did his mom put up with him? On the other hand — no Griffen, no car.

Rocket pulled on his elbow pads, sweater and helmet, grabbed his stick and went out. He took a few quick strides, then let himself glide on one skate, dragging his left toe behind him.

He'd been thinking about the Bowmont Blues. He'd make the team, play for a few games — say a third of the season — then call a bunch of AAA teams to see who needed a centre, had trouble scoring or needed help to make the playoffs. There could be a problem getting a release from the Blues, but hopefully not. He'd need a strong finish to the season to prove to Barker that he could still play. Maybe he'd even get lucky and grow a little. Then this whole thing would go away and he'd be the Rocket again.

The other players were circling the ice, talking in groups of two or three. He didn't know anyone and, feeling self-conscious about his shoulder pads, he kept to himself, careful not to skate next to anyone too long.

He passed one group. "I heard that he . . ." Rocket strained to listen, but he was going too fast. Were they talking about him? He shook his head and turned the corner, digging his edges in to pick up speed. He was being dumb. No one knew him.

Before he had time to circle the ice again, a tall woman came onto the ice, stick in hand. She blew her whistle and waved her stick overhead. The players laughed and joked around as they drifted over. It was painful to watch the guys on the team goofing off because they'd made it and had nothing to worry about. He quickly counted the bodies: twenty skaters, including him. Assuming three lines and three sets of defence, that meant five guys were getting cut tonight.

"Welcome to those of you who are new, and welcome back to those of you who have come to the other two tryouts. I'm the coach of the Blues, Sonia Duplain-Contreras — but that's a bit of a mouthful, so everyone calls me Coach Sonia. We're lucky enough to have a parent helping out, but he couldn't make it tonight, so you'll meet him later.

"I know tryouts are an unpleasant side of competitive hockey. I don't take the decisions lightly. I also don't think I'm always right. If we can't offer you a spot with the Blues this season, it doesn't mean you won't find another team. I've cut kids who've gone on to play AAA. All I can promise is to be honest and tell you what I think."

She was no Barker, at least.

Coach Sonia continued. "I want to give the new kids a real chance to show their stuff, so we won't be doing a ton of skating exercises." A group of three boys cheered. "Maybe an extra lap for you guys," she said. The boys booed. "So those in red, line it up on the goal line, blue, in behind. We'll whirl around a bit before we do a few skill drills — then a scrimmage. Okay?"

The players tapped their sticks on the ice and headed to the goal line. As Rocket skated past the coach, she tapped him on the arm. She looked briefly at his shoulders.

"Sorry, but I didn't meet you when you came in. What's your name?"

"Bryan Rockwood. My lift was late and . . ."

"Don't worry about it. You're here. Your friend Greg, I believe you played with his son, had some nice things to say about you," she said. "I'm looking forward to seeing you play."

Greg must have told her he'd played for the Huskies. Did he tell her why he was cut?

"Line 'er up, Bryan." She pointed with her stick.

He skated to the goal line, his stick across his knees. He needed to bring it, big time.

"Move it, Bryan!" the coach yelled.

The rest of Red was already halfway to the blue line. He'd been daydreaming and the drill had started.

Rocket took off like a racehorse bursting from the gate. The other players stopped at centre and turned back to the blue line, and he was forced to slow down so he wouldn't run into anyone. By the time he got back to top speed, they were long gone. He managed to catch one guy just before he crossed the far goal line.

He rested his stick across his knees head down. "You're blowing it, Rockwood," he muttered. "Bring it!"

Blue finished its drill and Rocket readied himself. The coach needed to see how he'd earned his nickname. The whistle blew.

After three strides, he was in front. He crossed the first blue line with a two-metre lead, stopping hard at centre, a spray of ice chips flying in his wake. With a quick stride, head down to gain speed, he was almost at the first blue line before some players had even entered the neutral zone.

Suddenly, he was flat on his back, staring up at the ceiling. A face peered down at him. "Hey, bro. Sorry. I didn't see you. You went right into my shoulder."

Another face came into view.

"My goodness, Bryan. Are you okay?" said Coach Sonia.

Hardly okay — humiliated more like it. An image of Kinger's mocking eyes appeared to him. He got to his knees.

"Stay down," said the coach. "Does your neck hurt?"

"I'm fine," he said. He did feel a bit groggy. He took a deep breath and rolled his neck a couple of times.

Coach Sonia put a hand on his shoulder and took a

good look into his eyes. "Are you having trouble focusing?"

"I'm fine," he said again. "I . . . stupid . . . I wasn't looking. No worries."

To make him feel more ridiculous, all the other players had gathered around.

"Follow my finger," said the coach, holding up her index finger.

"I'm okay!" This was getting irritating.

"Are you dizzy at all?"

"No."

"Keep focused on my finger, please." Coach Sonia moved it back and forth. After a minute, she put her glove back on. "I think it would be wise to shut it down for tonight and see if you have any concussion symptoms. You took a good shot, and I don't want to take any risks."

Shut it down? He'd barely gotten started. In a state of rising panic, he said, "I don't have a concussion. I'm fine, look." He shook his head from side to side.

A few of the guys laughed.

"Hockey players always say they're fine after a big hit," she said. "I didn't exactly see it, but I think your head might've collided with André's shoulder. Better safe than sorry, anyway. You'd best go to the dressing room. I really can't let you play until I know you don't have a concussion."

Rocket stared up at her. A gross, sick feeling rose up from his stomach and, for a moment, he thought he might actually throw up.

The coach patted Rocket on the back. "Don't get undressed right away. I want to talk to you for a sec, okay? I just need to explain the drill and then I'll come in." She skated off, calling, "We're going to do some figure eights, gentlemen, so line up in the right corner."

Rocket shuffled to the door in a daze. He hadn't made the team.

He pushed the blue plastic dot to open the door. It wouldn't budge. He jabbed at it with the butt-end of his stick a few times, and then he gave the door a shove with his hip.

"Stupid door. C'mon!" he yelled. He whacked the door with his stick.

"Hold on. Don't go mental." Maddy opened the door.

He pushed past her toward the dressing room.

"Where're you going?"

"She thinks I have a stupid concussion. Ordered me off — like I'm made of glass!"

Maddy followed along. "But why'd that guy hit you? Wasn't it a skating drill?"

She could be so annoying.

"He didn't hit me. I wasn't looking. Doesn't matter. I'm done. Didn't make the team — ten-second tryout. Such a *loser*." He pushed open the dressing room door. "I have to get changed. See you in front in five."

He kicked the door shut and flopped on the bench, ripping the straps off his helmet and flinging it into his bag. Then he took off his sweater and ripped his makeshift shoulder pads off, stuffing them into his bag. Dumbest idea ever — *towels*! He began to undo his sock tape. There was a knock on the door. Now what?

"Yah?" he called.

Coach Sonia popped her head in. "Hold up. I wanted to talk to you for a second before you got dressed." She came in. "Are you really sure you're not dizzy or disoriented?"

"I feel like normal," he said. "Sorry about this. You should get back to the tryout."

"I just wanted to talk to you for a minute. Greg told me about the Huskies. Must be hard not being able to play with your friends."

So he'd told her. Great. Totally embarrassing.

"It was . . . Whatever. Nothing I can do about it."

"Did you try out for other teams?"

"Yeah, a few."

"AAA teams?"

Rocket rolled the tape from his shin pad into a ball and tossed it into the garbage can. "I went to a Wilmont tryout," he said quietly.

"Any AA?"

"By the time we called around, most of the spots were taken — or maybe they couldn't find teams that wanted me. I'm not sure . . ." His voice trailed off.

"I'll tell you what. There's not a boy on this team who can skate like you. I watched you during the warm-up, and in the last drill you went from the goal line to centre like a rocket."

He had to smile at that.

"Greg told me a lot about you — your competitive-ness, your leadership — and the goals and assists. He's a big fan. Said in his opinion you were the best player on the team."

Rocket looked up at her. That surprised him. Greg

was probably just being nice, but still — he didn't have to say those things.

"I admire your courage for coming out tonight," she continued. "It says a lot about you — not giving up. I respect that a great deal. It's certainly unfortunate that your tryout ended before it began, but I'm going to let you in on a secret."

He waited.

"I'd decided to offer you a spot on the team after talking to Greg and checking out your stats from last season. I should be honest with you: we had a difficult year. I didn't think we were ready, but the parents pushed hard for it, so we moved up to AA. We didn't win a regular season game, although we got close a few times by the end of the year. We could really use a player with your offensive game and your speed. Even more than that, we could use a kid who has a passion for the game. We have skill on this team. We do. But sometimes the boys don't fight hard enough to win. I blame myself. I'm their coach and it's my job to get it out of them. So far, I haven't been able to. Anyway, if you're willing to drop down to this level, I'd love to have you."

Rocket had trouble taking it in. "You're offering me a spot? Even after that? You didn't even see me play."

She peered down at him. "Tell me, am I making a mistake? I need a centre who can dominate both ends of the ice, and who has the drive to play hockey the way it's supposed to be played. You up for it?"

He took a deep breath. "Yes."

"Who brought you?" she said.

"A neighbour, from my building. My mom had to work."

"No problem. I'll get you the forms. Can you hang around a bit? I need to get back out there, but I'll find the paperwork when I have a break." She pushed the door open and looked back. "You'll look good in blue, Bryan," she said.

The door closed.

He began to untie his skates.

The Bowmont Blues.

Maybe he should've just quit.

Dominate at both ends. Play the right way.

Maybe?

CHAPTER 15

Rocket closed the trunk and hopped into the back seat with his sticks. "Thanks for the lift, Griffen. Sorry it took so long." Rocket grinned at Maddy and she turned to look out the window so Griffen wouldn't see her laugh.

"Eight-thirty already," Griffen growled. "Complete waste of a night, and I knew the traffic was going to be brutal."

He'd been fuming about the time and the traffic since they left the rink. It was cool of him to drive, obviously, but it was hard to be thankful when the guy was such a jerk about it. Still, Rocket had to be nice because his mom would need to borrow the car for hockey sometimes — maybe lots of times. He sure hoped he could hook into a carpool, or it would be a long, long season.

"Hey, Mads. You want to come over and watch TV?"

"She's got homework," Griffen said.

"No, I don't," Maddy said. "I did it at the rink."

"You watch too much TV."

"Just for an hour, to relax. No big deal."

Griffen snorted. Then, after a long pause, said, "I need you to clean the kitchen before you go. There are dishes in the sink and the floor's dirty. Don't stay too long, either. I'll probably be going out with Risa, and I want you home first."

Rocket bit his lower lip and squeezed his stick. He really hated when his mom went out with Griffen, whatever "going out" meant. She was probably only going because Griffen had given him a ride. Now he felt guilty. But how else was he supposed to get to hockey? They drove the rest of the way in silence, forced to listen to Griffen's favourite radio station.

Griffen parked the car in the underground lot.

"I have to throw my equipment in the storage locker," Rocket told Maddy.

Griffen wrinkled his nose. "You ever wash your stuff? Smells like someone died in there. I don't want your stinky bag smelling up my vehicle, okay? You get it cleaned. I'm no taxi."

"Okay, Griffen. I'll get it dry-cleaned," Rocket said. As if!

Maddy stifled a giggle.

Rocket took his bag by the handle and waved his stick. "Thanks again, Griffen. See ya later, Maddy."

Griffen marched off. Behind him, Maddy giggled outright, covering her mouth with her hand.

"Hurry up," Griffen shouted back to her. "You're going nowhere until that kitchen shines."

"I'll be over in five minutes," she whispered, before running to catch up with Griffen.

Rocket wheeled his bag to the locker, undid the lock

and put his stuff up on the shelf. He ran to the elevator, hoping to catch them, but they'd left and he had to wait a long time for the next one.

Poor Maddy. One night with Griffen felt like a lifetime. What was it like for her? He hoped his mom got out of meeting him tonight. She usually came up with some excuse.

When the elevator doors opened, he could hear the old couple in 1203 arguing, as usual. It hadn't been too bad lately, not like two months ago when the cops were called. And 1207's TV was about normal — absolutely blaring.

His mom was reading on the couch when he came in. She nodded toward her bedroom. "I think they've figured out a way to attach the television to their stereo," she said.

"1203 is going at it, too," he said.

"I asked the super *again* for an apartment on another floor. As usual, he just smiled and nodded. Yesterday a new family moved into 606 and he never offered it to me. I know he wants me to bribe him, but someone told me the going rate is a thousand. Where am I going to get that?"

"It's not so bad here."

"Yeah? Well, I've been looking at some other buildings, but the rent in this city is atrocious. How can anyone afford to live here? I know we can't. If your dad actually paid his child support, then maybe . . ."

He knew she'd mention that as soon as the topic of money came up.

"Maddy's coming over to watch TV for a bit. Is that okay?"

"Do you have any homework this weekend?"

"Nah."

"That's what you always say."

"Honest. I don't. "

"Fine. What happened at the tryout? How'd it go?"

"Good, I guess. Maybe more like weird. I ran into someone during a drill — my fault for not keeping my head up — and the coach freaked out about a concussion."

His mother sat up, her face white as a sheet. "Bryan! You got a concussion? Oh, my goodness. That's it for hockey. Do you have any idea how dangerous that is? It can affect you later in life: headaches, forgetfulness, mood swings, depression . . ."

"Mom! I'm fine. I don't have a concussion. The coach told me she was just being super cautious. Relax. You've told me a hundred times about concussions. I'm not dizzy, tired, nauseous — nothing."

She came over and looked into his eyes. "Can you focus? Any blurry vision? Do you remember where you hit your head?"

"I said I was fine. I didn't hit my head."

She put him through a series of tests, making him touch his nose rapidly with his index fingers, balance on one foot, repeat number sequences. He didn't complain. He knew it would be over faster if he just did it.

She hugged him. "You seem to check out. Play your silly hockey."

"Thanks, Mom."

"So you got hit and left the ice. Where did that leave things?"

"That's the weird part. Coach came into the dressing

room and offered me a spot, even though I was literally on the ice for seven minutes. I'm officially a Bowmont Blue, or I will be when you sign the contract. Here are some forms to fill out." He handed them over sheepishly, because they were all folded and one page was ripped.

His mom rolled her eyes and took the forms. "Typical Bryan condition. But, anyway, congrats! Do you know where they practise?"

"I think there's a letter explaining all that." He pointed to the forms.

"I'm proud of you, Bryan. Did you meet any of the boys on the team? Are they a good group?"

"Not really sure. I got there kind of late and then, like I said, I wasn't on the ice long."

She shook her head angrily. "Did Griffen get the time wrong again? I told him to come at six."

"He said he was held up at work and there was traffic. I got on the ice when the tryout started, but barely."

"That guy . . ." She rolled her eyes.

"He said you were going out with him tonight?"

Her face fell. "I said I might, but I'm tired. Don't feel like it."

"So don't. Me and Maddy don't have to watch TV."

She smiled. "Thanks, dear. But . . . he did drive you and . . . Anyway, no matter. I might go out for a bit just to get away from that TV blasting in my ear."

"We can switch bedrooms if you want. The noise doesn't bother me."

She patted him on the shoulder. "I'm going to get ready. You take a shower first."

"I only played for a few minutes."

"Whatever. You put on that equipment and the stink transfers onto you. Besides, you have a lady friend coming over."

"It's just Maddy."

"Go!"

He went to the bathroom and turned on the shower. The water felt good, and he closed his eyes and let it bounce off his head and shoulders. The Bowmont Blues. Was he making a stupid mistake? Should he wait? Spots did open in September sometimes, although not really at AAA. He was kind of fooling himself there. But drop down? Would he ever get back? What was this coach like? Did she know her hockey?

With so many questions racing through his head, it was hard to enjoy the shower.

He got out and ran a hand over the mirror to wipe away the mist. The face of a little kid looked back. Some boys in grade seven had hairy legs and a bit of a moustache already, and then there was him. He could pass for a grade four. He turned away in disgust and got dressed.

Wandering back to the living room, he saw his mom and Maddy sitting on the couch together.

"That was fast," he said to Maddy.

"I . . . There wasn't much to do." Her eyes looked a little red and puffy. "I've been here for a few minutes."

"I was taking a shower, even though I didn't need one," Rocket joked.

His mom slapped Maddy's knee and got up. "We'll pick this up another day," she said to her. "Bryan, I had a quick look through the forms. I hope we can find other parents to give you a lift. Otherwise, I don't know what we'll do. The home rink is far, like an hour away, without traffic. A seven o'clock game would be a nightmare."

"We'll figure it out. I'm sure there's someone. I think the first practice is this Wednesday."

She stared wide-eyed out the window. "I have a shift Wednesday. I'll ask Griffen if he can help out. Anyway . . . excuse me." She went to her bedroom.

"What were you guys talking about?" he said.

Maddy crossed her legs. "Nothing. Just stuff. How was the shower?"

He sat on the other side of the couch. "The shower was hot and soapy. Very unusual."

"At least you took one — that's a first."

"Hey, I'm a new man." He waited for a sec. "Everything okay?"

"Yeah."

"Are you sure?"

"Yes, Bryan," she said forcefully.

"Cool. Anyway, it was nice of Griffen to drive me, even with the complaining."

"Yeah. He's awesome."

That's all he needed to hear. They must have had a fight, which they did all the time. He didn't understand Griffen. Maddy was as close to a perfect kid as you could get. She was a genius at school, got all A's and never got in trouble. He got that Griffen hadn't signed up to be her dad, and it wasn't his fault Maddy's mom took off like that. But it wasn't Maddy's fault, either.

"I think my mom's going out with him tonight." He followed her eyes to his mom's bedroom. "They're not . . ."

"I doubt it, but how freaky would that be?"

They both fell quiet and then burst out laughing.

"Hey, sis! Are you stoked about our family camping trip?" he said in an excited, happy voice.

"Sure am, bro. Let's have a family game of crazy eights."

"Not until we have our family pillow fight."

As quickly as it started, the joke stopped being funny.

"Would TV solve your problems?" he said.

"Absolutely every single one of them," she said.

He flicked the set on and punched in a number. "Perfect. The game's not over." He dropped to the floor and began to do sit-ups.

"Are you serious?" she said.

"About?"

"I'm supposed to sit here and watch hockey, which I don't really like, while you do sit-ups, which I don't really get."

"I didn't do my sit-ups this morning," he said. At thirty, he switched to side crunches.

She dropped to the floor and leaned forward. "I know you love hockey. Trust me. I get it. But don't you think you're a bit obsessed? Like, you just had a tryout, it's nine-thirty, and you're doing sit-ups and watching more hockey."

He sat up. "Weren't you the one who told me not to quit?"

"I'm not saying quit. Play. But, Bryan, come on. It's fun to think about the NHL and all that, and I guess all guys do when they're young. You're not a little kid any-more, and maybe you need to be more realistic."

"Realistic? Because I'm a shrimp, you mean? Too tiny to play with the big boys? Thanks. I'll prove you wrong, and Kinger and Adam and Ty and Barker, too — all of you."

Eyelids half-shut, Maddy let out a sigh and said, "It's not easy being your sister."

Rocket began his crunches on the other side. "I'll get you box seats, sis, but not all the time. I have important friends."

Maddy hopped back on the couch and tucked her legs under her. "I want front row, behind your bench, so I can tell you what to do."

Rocket's stomach was beginning to ache. He reached forty and lay down to catch his breath.

"Can you explain it?" she said quietly. "Just once, and I promise not to ask again."

He sat up and stared at the TV. He'd never tried to put it in words before, why he was only really happy on the ice, where everything made sense — or at least it had until he got cut from the Huskies. He turned the game off, the only sound coming from the neighbour's television.

"You're so smart, Maddy, and you have tons of friends. You'll be a doctor or a lawyer or something awesome. What am I going to do? I'm no brainiac like you. How am I going to get away from this place? I don't want to live in this stupid, smelly building all my life, and I want to help my mom so she doesn't have to work all the time. Hockey is all I've got — it's the only thing I'm good at. And when I'm skating and playing, I feel like I don't have any problems. It's like life is better on the ice. Plus, it's my only shot. I'm sure of it.

Otherwise, I'll be stuck in this neighbourhood forever — a total loser — another Grady," he finished bitterly.

"You're not going to turn out like Grady."

"Why not?" he said. "He had a chance to make the NHL, to be rich and respected, but instead he got hurt and has nothing."

"I think it's more complicated than that," Maddy said. "It's not like you become a street person if you don't make the NHL."

"No kidding — I'm not that stupid. And I don't think everyone who lives here is a loser, but you know what I mean: the gangs, the garbage, the street people — Grady!" He looked her in the eye. "I'm good, Maddy. Really good. I know it's a long shot, but why not? I want it and I can play the game. I was the league's lead scorer last year — in AAA — the lead scorer. But one idiot coach decided I was too small and no one else wanted me. I'm not going to be washed up at thirteen." He slapped the floor with his fist.

"You're not just a hockey player, Bryan."

He began to do more sit-ups.

She was wrong. Dead wrong.

Without hockey, he was nobody — a nobody going nowhere.

CHAPTER 16

Rocket stopped in front of the door to calm his nerves. He'd played in plenty of big games, finals in tournaments, league championships. But he'd never been more scared than he was right now, about to start his first practice with the Blues.

"That's the right door."

He flushed. "Hi, Coach. I couldn't remember if it was three or four."

"It's three," she said. "Tell the boys I want them dressed in ten minutes, then I'm coming in."

Rocket pushed the door. The guys were talking to each other; there was lots of laughing. It sounded like a typical hockey dressing room. It was also the sound of guys who knew each other, which meant he was most definitely an outsider.

The first problem was finding a seat. Griffen had been late, as usual, and the room was full. Rocket leaned his sticks against the wall and took a few steps forward. He looked like an idiot, and he knew it.

"There's a spot over here," said a kid, pulling his bag over and sliding to the side to make room.

It was the same kid he'd run into at the tryout — André. Rocket sat, unzipped his bag, pulled out his pants and began hunting around for his jock.

The volume level dropped slowly, until no one was really talking much. Rocket snuck a peek as he put on his shin pads. All eyes were on him. He struggled to think of something to say to break the ice. He prayed he wasn't turning red.

"How's the noggin?" André said to him.

Rocket sat up and touched his temple. "I'm good. I don't think I hit my head. Stupid of me — I wasn't looking where I was going."

"Coach Sonia's a fanatic about concussions — likes us to play hard, though."

"You played for her last year?"

He nodded, his smile slightly cockeyed. "Most of us did. We started together in select and then A and last year up to AA . . ."

"Make something up," a fair-haired boy said from across the room.

A few of the boys began to laugh.

"Why bother? We can't do worse this year," André said. All the guys laughed this time. "But you may as well tell him, Noah."

Noah, the fair-haired boy, looked disgusted. "You all think it's funny, and Coach Sonia tells us to just have fun, but we only won one game all year, and that was in a tournament."

"Coach isn't like that," André said. "She wants us to win. We all do. It was only our first year in AA. We'll be ready this season."

Rocket pulled on his pants and began to tape his

socks. One win — at least that was one more than he'd thought.

Somehow that didn't make him feel better.

There was a lull, and then another kid piped up. "You played AAA, right?"

It was the goalie. Rocket was startled. He hadn't expected someone to come right out and ask.

"I did."

"You guys any good?" the goalie said.

"Good question, Dominic," said the kid next to him.

"Thanks, Blake," Dominic said, and they punched fists.

Obviously, they'd been talking about him. They may as well know the entire story. "We might've won more than one game."

"Did you snag two?" Blake said.

"Think so," Rocket said.

They were all looking at him. He waited and then shrugged. "We might've won the championship."

That broke everyone up.

"We could use a bit of that action," Noah said.

"Welcome to the Blues, bro," André drawled. He was grinning as he held out his hand, and they shook.

"Any other new guys on the team?" Rocket said.

"Nope," said Dominic.

He was the only new player on the worst team in the league? It was laugh or cry time. He decided to laugh. "This new guy better be good," he said.

The room erupted. When it quieted down, Dominic asked the dreaded question. "So why'd you drop down?"

"I don't blame you, bro," Blake said. "I got a bud who plays for the Sharks, and you'd think he was in the NHL. He's on the ice six times a week, tournaments practically every weekend, paid coaches, crazed parents. Who needs it?"

"It's intense, for sure," Rocket said. "Lots of hockey. The new Huskies coach is definitely a lunatic."

"Is that why you're playing for us?" Dominic persisted.

Out of the corner of his eye, Rocket noticed André give Dominic a stern look.

"It was that and . . . other stuff."

The door opened and Coach Sonia walked in.

"I'd like to officially welcome everyone onto the team, this being our first practice and all," she said. "I'm excited for the season and I hope we all have lots of fun — and learn a little something along the way."

"And win more than one game!" Noah said.

"That would be nice," she said. "We improved a lot last year, especially in the last third of the season. Don't get down on yourselves. If we work hard at practice and improve each game, the wins will come. They will."

Rocket could tell the boys liked their coach. They listened to her — like he used to listen to Coach Neilson.

"I do want to talk about a few things," she continued. "First, is the way we practise. Maybe last season we didn't always concentrate enough. Teams play games like they practise. I want you all to think about paying the price during practice; that will translate into wins. Second, we're going to increase our fitness level. That was a problem last season. So you have summer homework: turn the computer or the TV off once in a while and do some sit-ups or go for a run — anything. We got tired in the third period. Okay?"

A chorus of "got ya" and "sure" answered.

Coach Sonia opened the door. "Zamboni's on. Let's get going."

Rocket rooted around in his bag for his shoulder pads. He hadn't quite finished dressing. His mom had not been happy to hear that he'd lost them. He pretended he'd left them in the dressing room at the try-out. No way he'd tell her about Raja; she'd flip out.

Fortunately, she'd tossed some old equipment in their storage locker thinking she'd sell it one day. Rocket had found his shoulder pads from his first year with the Huskies. They were tight, but he could slip them on. They looked ridiculous, of course, and his mom had burst out laughing when he'd tried them on. She said she'd buy him new ones, but she needed time to save money, unless they could find a good used pair.

How sweet would it be to get Raja on the ice for even one minute, one forecheck? He'd hit him so hard the boards would shake for a month.

Rocket's teammates began to file out. He didn't relish the idea of them seeing his pathetic little-kid shoulder pads. Fiddling around with his skates, he stalled while they cleared out. Hopefully, he'd have new pads by the weekend.

André was looking for something in his bag, and as each kid left, Rocket's anxiety level grew. André was dressed. What was he looking for? The last kid left and André got up.

"I hope you don't think you joined a bunch of

losers," André said. "We can win. We only need some guys to get a bit more serious and, like Coach Sonia said, we're going to work on that. She's a good coach, you'll see. Played on our National team. Knows more about hockey than anyone I've ever met. As for the Blues, we weren't ready to move up last year. We are now." André looked so serious and intense; Rocket had to force himself not to laugh.

"We should get out there," André said.

Life was one big pain. Couldn't he go already? Then inspiration hit. "Is the Zamboni off? It's a stupid superstition of mine: can't leave the room until it's off the ice. Dumb, I know but . . ."

"I'll check it out," André said, and he turned toward the door.

Quick as a flash, Rocket stuffed his pads over his head, followed by his sweater to cover them up. He reached for his elbow pads.

"Is that another superstition?" André said, watching as Rocket put his elbow pads on under his sweater.

"I know. I'm pathetic. I started putting my elbow pads on like this in house league," Rocket said to cover up. "Now I think there'll be a zombie apocalypse if I don't."

"Do it then," André said. "The season will get real messed if we have to deal with zombies."

"Hockey stick is a good weapon with zombies," Rocket said.

"I'd go with a baseball bat. That's assuming zombie skulls are mushy. If they're hard like ours, then you'd probably want a sword or a gun," André said with a grin.

Rocket put on his helmet, snapped up the face mask

and grabbed his gloves. "Go Blues," he said.

André slapped Rocket's shin pads. "We do 'Go Big Blue!' Intimidates the other team — or, that's what we tell ourselves."

"Works for me," Rocket said. He took his stick and gave André's shin pads a tap. "After you."

André looked at him. "And you have to be the last guy on the ice?"

"Sorry."

Laughing, André went out first. Rocket could only shake his head. Goodbye Rocket: hello Superstition Kid. All because of that Raja idiot. He hopped onto the ice and took off up the side wall, swaying his shoulders from side to side to loosen up.

Last place.

Same players.

Go Big Blue!

CHAPTER 17

The whistle blasted.

Rocket slammed on the brakes at the blue line, snow spraying, controlling the puck with the tip of his blade. André and Reid continued drifting backward. On his right, Noah curled slowly to a stop. Blake put his stick across his knees and continued gliding forward.

The whistle blasted again. Coach Sonia skated toward them.

Rocket was a bit surprised. She could really motor.

"When the whistle blows, I need you to stop right away," she yelled.

This was a different Coach Sonia — a lot less motherly.

"One player stopped immediately — Bryan!" she said.

He wished she wouldn't single him out. She'd already done that during a skating drill. He'd been out in front and she told them all to watch how hard he worked. Last thing he wanted was to be pegged the coach's pet.

"You know why Bryan stopped?" the coach said.

No one answered.

"Blake, do you know?"

He shook his head.

"Noah? André? Reid? Anyone? What about you, Bryan? Why did you stop like that?" she said.

He had no idea what to say.

"Let me ask it another way. What would happen in a Huskies practice if the coach blew his whistle and you didn't stop right away?

Rocket had to laugh. It meant a whole lot of pain. "The entire team would probably have to do suicides for ten minutes — or, if you were lucky, you'd only have to sit on the bench for a few drills."

Rocket suddenly realized he'd said something incredibly stupid. Coach Sonia would make them do suicides — and it would be his fault. Coach Neilson's suicides had been brutal: sprint to the blue line, drop to their knees, get up and skate to the red line, back to the blue and then all the way to the other end. First five times were fun — the next twenty were brutal. What a great way to meet your teammates at the first practice!

The coach turned to the rest of the team. "Did you hear that? It's been drilled into him for years, after countless practices. Whistle: stop! Whistle: stop!" Her face was red and her tone was angry. The other kids drifted closer to listen. "If you don't immediately stop on the whistle, you won't be in the right spot to see the problem. Like on that rush — Bryan was going to dump the puck into the right corner, but Noah had slowed down and was too far back. He wouldn't have beaten Reid to the puck. But I can't show him that now because Noah skated for another two metres after the whistle."

"Sorry," Noah said.

"Don't be sorry," Coach Sonia snapped. "Do it next time. Because this is an example of what's wrong with our game. We don't do things seriously, over and over, until they're second nature. Things like having two hands on the stick, moving our feet and going hard on the puck — a good player practises these until he doesn't have to think about them anymore: he just reacts. Then it's fast, it's direct, it's efficient. We're always a half-second too slow, because we think too much, or because we don't practise at a high tempo."

"We're *very* sorry," Blake joked.

"Smarten up!" she said. Her eyes looked like they'd pop out of her head. "Jokes and fun are great, but — news flash — this isn't the time."

Blake remained perfectly still.

Rocket had the impression this was a side of Coach Sonia the team didn't see often.

"And the conditioning?" she said.

There was apparently no stopping her now.

"Has anyone noticed the slight difference between Bryan's fitness level and theirs? Who do you think is going to dominate in the third period, or at the end of a long shift? We are absolutely not in good enough shape." She stopped for a moment, then nodded. "Okay . . . hissy fit is over. But we definitely need to step it up. I simply cannot lose every game again next season. It'll kill me."

"You won one game," Rocket said.

The words had just come out without thinking. He felt like an idiot.

Everyone began laughing, including Coach Sonia. Rocket didn't know what to do — so he joined in.

"You know what, Coach?" André said. "Maybe those suicides aren't such a bad idea."

"Let's do it," Noah said.

Blake laughed. "I can't believe I'm saying this, but okay." Then, looking at Dominic, he asked, "Hey, Bryan. Did goalies do suicides on the Huskies?"

"Yeah," Rocket said. "Why not?"

Blake let out a huge roar. Dominic stared blankly at Rocket — and then he laughed.

"I guess I could be fitter, too," Dominic said.

"You guess?" Blake said. "You're like a beach ball."

"I'll beat you down the ice, Mr. Slow Motion," Dominic said.

"I like the spirit," the coach said. "Everyone down at the far end."

Twenty minutes later Rocket dragged himself off the ice with his teammates. Sonia had obviously heard of suicides, too — she'd even thrown in a few new variations, including ten push-ups at each blue line. After three rushes, his arms ached. He'd done pretty well, though, winning virtually every rush.

"You're lucky I can't breathe, André. Otherwise, I'd have to kill you for telling Coach that we need suicides," Blake said. He flopped onto the dressing room bench and lay down.

"I did it for you," André said.

The rest of the team trudged in and threw themselves down.

Blake sat back up. "Actually, I think it's Bryan's fault."

Rocket felt a rush down his spine. They were going to blame him. This happened with the Huskies — they always made life miserable for one kid every year.

"You have to stop working so hard," Noah said. "Makes us look like . . ."

"Like we're not working very hard?" Blake said.

"If it means we don't lose every game this season, I'm in," André growled.

"Hey, I didn't say I wasn't going to do it," Blake said. "I'm just going to complain about it."

Dominic came in and fell on the floor. "Kill me now. It's only a matter of time until I die."

"I thought we'd kill André first, but okay. Can you wait for me to get my samurai sword — I like how the blade takes a head off — less splatter," Blake said.

"Splatter's the best part, bro," Dominic said. "I'd prefer if you took me out with a hammer."

Rocket grinned at their banter.

"No worries," Blake said to his friend, his face full of compassion. "I'd be happy to smash your head in with a hammer. I've got a sledgehammer in the car that could do the trick in one hit."

"I'm in," Dominic said.

The door opened and a man came in.

"Is there a Bryan Rockwood here?" he said.

"Hey, Dad," Blake said.

Rocket held his hand up.

"Your dad's in the lobby and he wants you to hurry up."

Blake's dad left. Rocket felt the blood rush to his face. He'd been having such a good time listening to Blake and Dominic, he'd forgotten Griffen and Maddy were waiting. He pulled his shoulder pads off with his hockey sweater so nobody would see them, and raced to get dressed.

"Dads always tell you to hurry up," Dominic said. "They never tell you why, though."

"I just ignore mine. It brings us closer together," Blake said.

"He's not my dad," Rocket said quickly.

The boys left him alone, but he noticed Blake and Dominic give each other a look. No time to worry about that. He pulled his sweatshirt on. "Good practice, guys. I'll see you at the exhibition game," he said.

A chorus of "see ya" rang out, plus one "slow down next practice" from Blake, which made him laugh. They were good guys. This dressing room had such a different feel to it. Sure, the Huskies had joked around and talked, but it was always competitive, like you always had to be careful of what you said or someone would burn you, and guys were always bragging about how they "dangled" someone or "roofed it." These guys — they just had fun.

Rocket went into the lobby.

"Get your butt outta there in less than two hours next time, or you'll walk home," Griffen snarled.

"Sorry. I . . . The coach went over some strategy."

"Like a girl's going to know strategy. Ridiculous team. Can't believe you bother. You should just quit." Griffen nodded at the door. "Hurry up, the two of you. Waste of a night." He muttered something under his breath and stomped off.

Maddy reached out and took his stick, and they followed Griffen.

"Would it be so wrong?" she said, motioning at Griffin with the stick.

She was smiling, as if it were a joke. It didn't seem that funny to him.

They pushed through the doors into the parking lot, both lost in their own thoughts.

CHAPTER 18

Rocket leaned back in his chair. This was brutal. Three days in a row of eating at his locker and hanging in the library doing homework. He'd never been so up to date on his assignments. The first day hadn't been too bad, but now it was killing him. To make it worse, looking out the window he could see the guys playing football. No one had told him about it, so no way was he going to show up — not with Kinger dying to burn him, Adam laughing at him and Ty . . . Well, Ty not doing anything. Rocket would rather eat lunch at his locker for the rest of the year — and grade eight, too — than hang with them.

Ty and Adam hadn't really said anything to him after he'd quit the Butt Kickers. He'd run into them a few times, of course. They'd say hi, and he'd asked them some lame question to do with school. But usually they avoided each other. It was less awkward to not talk. It was funny: he used to think he had a ton of friends. Now he wasn't sure he had any.

So here he was, holed up in the library. Bored, he put his pencil between his thumb and his first finger and tried to spin it around through his fingers. It went flying across the table and onto the floor.

"Are you mad at your pencil or practising a self-defence move?"

Rocket looked over.

"Hey, Megan. Didn't see you there." She was wearing jeans and a sweatshirt again. This time her hair hung down naturally, thick and wavy.

She opened her eyes wide and nodded. "Okay. I'll buy that. Your pencil?"

He smiled sheepishly. "I was trying to spin it on my fingers. Got to work on it, I guess."

"You mean like this?" she said. She picked up the pencil, held it between her fingers and began to spin it around and around without stopping.

"Very cool trick," he said. "Where'd you learn to do that?"

"Years of geek training," she said. "It's compulsory."

"Well, um, it's a cool trick."

She gave the pencil back. "I've been looking for you. You missed practice yesterday."

"Practice?"

"You've forgotten the trivia team already?"

He hadn't forgotten; he just hadn't bothered to look for them.

"Come on. We've got half an hour," she said. "We're finishing up with some geography and then we can get to sports."

She said it like he had no choice.

And it was better than nothing.

"So Nigel was telling us you're quite the hockey player," she said.

"Don't know about that. I play."

She pushed the door open for him.

"Thanks."

They walked down the hall.

"I bet the boys would be pretty happy if you played on their floor hockey team," she said. "They love to play, but the other teams seem to be . . . better. Bird has a friend who played with them last year, but he's busy doing the lighting for the school play. They wanted me to play but, frankly, no."

She stopped and looked at him. "I mean, do I look like a floor hockey player?"

She didn't really look like anything to him — other than a girl, of course. But some of them played floor hockey, too. "I don't know. Maybe?"

Megan scrunched her eyebrows. "I *maybe* look like a floor hockey player?"

"No," he said hurriedly. "Maybe I'll play. Maybe."

That was so not going to happen.

She opened a door.

"Capital of Mali?" Des asked.

"Bamako," Bird said.

"Capital of Angola?" Des asked.

"Luanda," Daniel said.

"Capital of Zambia?"

"Lusaka," Nigel said.

"Capital of Senegal?"

"Dakar," Megan called out.

Four heads spun around.

"Oh, okay. It's Bryan, right?" Bird said.

"Uh, I was in the library . . ."

"My fault," Megan said. "I forgot to tell Bryan

about the practice, so no harm. He's here now. I rescued him from a flying pencil. He could've been killed." She put a hand on his shoulder. "Don't feel you have to thank me. I was happy to do it."

"I owe you," Rocket said.

Nigel's face was hard and angry. Arms crossed, he glared at Rocket. "Things are organized," Nigel said. "We don't need another player."

"We could always use the help," Bird said.

"We're allowed six," Des said. "And we voted."

"So what? We're good with five; we don't need a one-trick pony on sports. It's stupid."

This was ten times worse than any library. "Okay. No worries," Rocket said.

His voice came out sounding sad. He was acting like a loser. Time to man up. "I don't need to be on the trivia team. I was just killing time."

"Don't be silly," Megan said. "We're always on the lookout for new members, and there's nothing wrong with a little extra expertise on the sports side. It'll let Nigel focus more on geography."

"We shouldn't be adding people before the first match," Nigel said.

"Why not?" Bird said.

Nigel pushed back in his chair. His eyes burned in fury, but they were also glossy, as if he were on the verge of losing his temper and crying at the same time. "I come here to get away from guys like him, and now he wants to join the trivia team?" He glared at Rocket. "I know what's going on. Don't think I don't. You're not part of the cool kids anymore, so you've decided to lower yourself to our level. That's totally it. I say no way.

Get your own team." Nigel was shaking with rage, his hands gripping his knees tightly.

Rocket was stunned. He'd barely said a word to Nigel in his life. "I never did anything to you," he began. "Why the—"

"No, not the Rocket!" Nigel cut in. "Not Ty or Adman or all the rest. You're all *so* nice." He leaned forward and pointed at Rocket. "My name's Nigel, not Big Red, and your crew has made my life a nightmare since I got here, so don't give me the Mr. Wonderful act."

Rocket started to get angry, too, but then he thought back to a gym class near the beginning of the year. They'd had to choose sides for a game of soccer, and Nigel was the last kid to be picked. Adam had made a big deal about having to pick him. He'd called him Big Dead, because, as Adam said, Nigel didn't move on the field. Another time, Nigel had been accepting an award at an assembly, and Adam called him Big Red the Egg Head, and then Eggie. Then last week . . .

Rocket stopped. There were too many times. And he may not have made fun of Nigel, but he'd done nothing to stop it. Nothing. In fact, he'd usually laughed along. He'd never thought about how Nigel felt, because he hadn't cared.

His face hot with shame, Rocket made himself look Nigel in the eye. He saw a lot of library time in his future.

"You're right, and I'm sorry," Rocket said. "I've been a jerk, and so have my friends. We thought we were being funny. I know it won't help, or maybe it won't make sense, but honestly, we weren't trying to be mean or bully you. We were just goofing on you, like we do to everyone. It's like we don't think about how it might bother other people. We just don't, as long as our friends laugh. That doesn't make it okay, I know. Anyway, you're right that me and those guys, well, we're not such good friends anymore." Rocket looked out the window. It had only been a few weeks, but his life had turned completely upside down.

"Why aren't you friends with those guys?" Bird said.

"It's kind of complicated."

They waited for him to continue.

Rocket sighed. "I was cut from a hockey team, the Huskies. I played on it with Ty and Ad-man, I mean Adam, and since I don't play in that league no more . . ."

"It's 'anymore,'" Nigel said.

"Shh!" Megan and Bird snapped.

Nigel flushed. "Well, it is," he murmured angrily.

"It's okay, Nigel," Rocket said. "I'm leaving." He turned and reached for the doorknob.

"Quick question, Bryan," Megan said. "Just so I get this straight, you're not friends with those guys anymore just because you don't play hockey with them?"

Rocket turned back, keeping his hand on the doorknob. "Like I said, it's complicated."

"I really don't get boys," she said.

"He has to be on the team," Bird said to Nigel. "He's a bigger misfit than you."

Des and Daniel burst out laughing.

"This is a special moment: our first member who can actually play hockey. This is historic," Bird said.

Megan lowered her head and looked at Nigel. "I think Bryan apologized," she said.

Nigel slowly uncrossed his arms. He looked down at the floor. "Okay. We could try it."

"I am sorry," Rocket said. He really was, and he tried to say it as sincerely as he could. He walked over, his hand extended. Nigel hesitated, then shook it.

"Should we finish up with the African geography?" Des said. "I have a few more questions, or do we want to move into sports since Bryan is here — or is it Rocket?"

"Bryan's good," he said.

"You may as well finish up the geography," Megan said.

Des began to fire out questions, and the others answered as fast as they could.

"The trick to this isn't to just know the answer," Megan whispered in Rocket's ear. "We practise to train our minds to think fast. Speed is the key, not the knowledge."

Rocket sat and listened, and every so often, a chuckle forced its way out. Bryan Rockwood was on the trivia team and playing hockey for the worst team in AA.

He looked over at Nigel. He couldn't imagine having to come to school every day scared that some kids were going to embarrass you in front of everyone.

Although, maybe he could imagine it now.

CHAPTER 19

Rocket kicked his skates forward in tiny steps as he waited for the other centre to line up. It was his way of fighting the nerves messing with his stomach.

He'd told himself over and over that this was just an exhibition game. Deep down, he knew that wasn't true. The boys were counting on him to produce. He'd felt them all looking at him in the dressing room. On the Huskies, he'd had Ty and Adam. Here, he was alone. Coach Sonia had even started him, with Blake on the left and Noah on the right.

They were probably the two best wingers on the team. They didn't have Ty's all-around game or Adam's wicked shot and, of course, the chemistry wasn't there. Still, they had skills. Noah was bent over, his stick on the ice, ready for the drop. He had the AAA intensity; Rocket would give him that. He worked hard, and his shot was okay, too. Foot speed needed work, maybe — he could lengthen his stride and not be so straight up-and-down. Blake was tougher to figure out. He had serious wheels and could handle the puck, but most of the time he barely put in an effort.

Usually, Rocket hated guys that didn't work hard. He liked Blake, though — he kept things loose and fun.

André and Reid were on defence. André wore the C, and apparently had for the past three years.

The whistle blew and the ref raised his arm to each goalie. The Toros goalie nodded. Dominic smacked his pads with his paddle. Rocket put his stick down and the ref held the puck out. Rocket shifted his left foot back ever so slightly to give himself more leverage to pull the puck back.

It dropped.

A roar sounded from behind the Blues bench. Rocket grunted in satisfaction as the puck spun to André on the right. The captain took a couple of steps to his right, and Rocket broke off in that direction. André rewarded him with a perfect snap pass. Rocket crossed the red line. The quick move had caught the forwards napping. Blake was still on the line and Noah hadn't moved either.

His first shift in his first game, Rocket didn't want to look like a hog, so instead of attacking he rolled into the middle of the neutral zone and slipped the puck off the boards in Blake's direction. The Toros right-winger out-hustled him for the puck, however, and was able to backhand it away. Reid was closest to the puck, so Rocket settled into an open spot two metres inside the red line and called for it.

Reid stayed rooted on the blue line.

"Reid!" Rocket shouted.

Too late. The Toros centre gathered the puck up. He took it hard at Reid and, a metre from the line, dumped it into the corner, shifting inside to get past him. André had anticipated the play and got to it first. Rocket figured he'd shovel it up the wall and he took off for the hash marks. Blake was still hanging outside the blue line.

"Use me, short-side," Rocket called.

André, showing skill Rocket hadn't known he had, pulled the puck toward his feet with the tip of his blade and, using the benefit of the angle, passed it to Rocket without bouncing it off the wall. Rocket whirled with the puck on his backhand into the high slot. Again, he had some clear ice ahead, but Noah had set up on the right side. When their eyes met, Rocket felt obliged and passed to him.

Then he cut across for the give-and-go. Noah snapped it over. Rocket took it in stride.

That was a Huskies-level breakout.

He took a few strides and sent it rink wide to Blake.

Rocket groaned. Okay, the guy was funny, but he was standing still. The pass missed him. The Toros right defenceman collected the puck inside his own end and swung it cross ice to his partner. He took off on a rush right up the middle. Blake lurked by the boards. He'll cut him off, Rocket thought, so he moved to his right figuring that was where the puck would end up.

Good plan, except Blake did little more than hold his stick out. The defenceman blew by him and bore down on the Blues defence. He faked an outside move, fooling Reid, and continued up the middle. André wasn't able to get over in time. Rocket couldn't believe his eyes. One against five, he'd beaten them all and now bore down on Dominic.

Dominic whacked his pads with his paddle and shuffled his feet, a weird habit Rocket had noticed before. It came at a bad time. The defenceman snapped a low drive to the stick side at that precise moment. The puck zipped into the corner. The Toros parents cheered and the players banged their sticks against the boards. The defenceman leapt into the air, a huge grin plastered across his face. He curled toward his teammates who had their gloves out.

Rocket wanted to smash his stick on the ice, but he couldn't risk breaking it. He was steaming mad: at Reid for getting beat, at Blake for being lazy and at Dominic for his little dance on the breakaway. He'd never been much for calling guys out, though, and he was the new guy. He kept his mouth shut and followed Blake and Noah off for a change.

"More aggressive on the puck," Coach Sonia said. "We can't let a guy stroll in on Dominic."

Rocket expected her to lose it, like she had at practice. The corners of her mouth were tight and pressed into a frown. She didn't say anything else, though.

"So did I tell you I got the new *Halo*?" Blake said to Noah. "I've been obsessed with it, and my mom caught me playing at three in the morning. She went nuclear and took my TV out of my room." He started laughing and so did Noah. "Like, I mean she took it right then and there, in the middle of the night. It's a monster, a fifty-incher, so she hauled my poor dad out of bed to help her. He was still half-asleep. They left my room and I heard a bang. The TV had decided to take a tumble down the stairs and smash into the wall. It made a big hole, too. Mom was so mad — she yelled at me for not lending a hand. I asked her why I should help them take away my TV."

Both boys were close to hysterics. Rocket thought it was funny, too, especially the way Blake told it. At the same time, it bugged him. They'd just given up a bad goal. It really wasn't the time for funny stories. He tortured himself over whether to say something.

"Hey, Bryan, what's up out there?"

André had come over.

"Tough way to start the game. We'll get it back," Rocket said.

"I had a total brain fart. Can't believe I let a stiff like that beat me," André said. "And I reminded Dominic not to do that stupid stick-pad thing before a breakaway. Coach was on him all last season about it. Anyway, what's with all the passing when you had a total chance to attack their D? When you have space, go for it."

Rocket didn't want to trash his linemates. "It's our first game together. The passing will come." It was an awkward conversation with Blake and Noah next to him.

André didn't care. "Feed Bryan the puck," he said to Rocket's two linemates. "They don't have a guy with his wheels. You boys get to the net for a rebound."

"Yeah. Sure," Blake said. "So, bro, did I tell you about my mom freaking out on my TV?"

"No. Later, okay? Focus on the game." André went back to the defence end of the bench.

A stick tapped Rocket's shin pads.

"Apparently, you have to win the game single-handedly. Do I need to do anything?" Blake said.

Rocket couldn't tell if he was serious or joking.

"Bryan, you're up," Coach Sonia snapped. "Wake up, boys!"

He felt like an idiot. The forwards were shifting. Shamefaced, he followed Noah and Blake to the faceoff circle on Dominic's left. Rocket adopted a reverse grip and glided slowly to the dot. He could do what André said and try to dominate, but Blake's comment stuck in his head.

The ref dropped the puck. The Toros centre swept the puck back to his right defenceman against the boards.

"I wasn't ready!" Rocket screamed. He jumped around the centre and pushed hard to get to the point.

"Stop daydreaming, number eighteen," the ref said.

The defenceman whistled a sharp pass across the line to his wide-open partner. Rocket's heart sank. Two shifts — two goals against? He couldn't let that happen.

The Toros left defenceman reared back. Rocket slid to the right. Fortunately, the shooter hesitated a moment, and that let Rocket get in front of him. He blasted the puck toward the net just as Rocket threw himself to the ice. The Toros parents groaned — a blocked shot. Rocket clutched his chest where the puck had deflected off him. The chest protection on his shoulder pads was thin, basically nothing more than a bit of material, and the shot really stung. But it hurt a lot less than a goal against. He scrambled to his feet. The puck was still in their zone. The Blues left defence-man, a kid named Matthew, was battling the Toros right-winger for possession in the left corner. The centre hovered in the high slot looking for a pass. Rocket skated to him and crossed his stick over the centre's to establish position.

"Get lost, little boy," the centre said, and he cross-checked him in the back.

"Idiot," Rocket shot back. He wasn't backing down to this jerk. "Ref, call it already."

The ref wasn't watching and the second ref wasn't even in the zone. Matthew won the puck and bashed it up the left wall to Blake at the hash marks. Their right defenceman pinched, his stick extended forward. Rocket elbowed the centre in the ribs and broke away.

"Use me, Blake," he called.

"See ya soon, squirt," the centre said.

Blake had other ideas. He kicked the puck to his stick and tried to curl around the defenceman with the puck on his backhand. The defenceman wasn't fooled, and he poke-checked the puck off Blake's stick. The right-winger lunged for the puck. Rocket was a hair quicker, and he reached out and snared it. Next, he turned to his left, thinking he'd be best off ringing the puck around the wall to Noah. The right-winger was a hustler, however, and he'd turned back and dashed in Noah's direction to cut him off. Just as quickly, Rocket changed direction, cutting hard on the inside edge of his left skate, and headed up ice. The right-winger swung his stick — too late.

"Heads up, little guy. I'm coming." The Toros centre was two metres away to his right.

Instinct took over. Rocket dipped his right shoulder, slid the puck between the centre's feet and spun counter-clockwise. The centre's elbow grazed his back, but that's all he got. Rocket collected the puck in the slot and powered forward. He took it all in: Blake, left, tied up with the right defenceman; Noah, covered by the left-winger; Toros left defenceman standing at the blue line; Toros centre and right-winger behind the play. It was a foot race.

Rocket exploded, pushing the puck forward with one hand. The left defenceman finally clued in and he turned and skated all out to get back. In three strides, they were even; by the red line, Rocket was a metre in front; by the blue line, he had a two-metre lead. The goalie was still deep in his crease. Rocket loved to deke when he was going this fast, especially on his forehand where he could slip it in the five-hole or roof it stick side. This situation screamed for a shot, however.

"Bring it," he said under his breath. He took another stride to the slot and snapped a wrister off his front foot, high to the stick side.

He slapped his stick on the ice and hopped up three times, his signature move when he scored. Sure, it was an exhibition game, but it felt good to see that hunk of rubber go in, and it made up for the first goal. His teammates came over and met him at the Toros' blue line. Noah had a confused look on his face, like he wasn't sure what to say. He tapped his shin pads.

"You're going to make André happy with that," Blake said, coming in behind Noah. "Those were some smoking wheels."

Rocket punched gloves with his other teammates and headed toward centre.

"That's the stuff, Rocket!" André yelled from the bench. He bashed the boards with his stick. A few parents clapped politely.

Rocket? How did André know about his nickname? It probably wasn't a good thing. The team would think he was showing off.

The same centre lined up. Rocket put his stick down. The centre slapped it away. Rocket ignored him. He did it again.

"Enough stick work," the ref said to the centre. "Once more and you're in the box."

The centre lowered his stick to the ice. "Crunch-body time, pygmy," he said to Rocket. "I wouldn't touch the puck again."

Rocket had been forced to deal with chirping about his size for years. He'd do more than touch the puck; he'd stuff it in the net. The ref dropped it. Rocket tapped it between the centre's legs and swerved around his left shoulder to sweep it up. Again, Noah and Blake were slow off the mark. No matter, he figured. He'd see what this defence pair was about.

The right defence was the guy who'd pinched against Blake. He'd been aggressive all game, too. Rocket went to him, dangling the puck forward with one hand. The right defenceman reached for it, but that made him lose his balance slightly; that was all the opportunity Rocket needed. Quick as a flash, he pulled the puck back to his forehand, and with two hard strides, he was outside the defenceman's right shoulder. The left defenceman couldn't get back in time. He had another clear-cut breakaway.

Again, the goalie hung back in his crease. If it's not broke, don't fix it, Coach Neilson always said. So Rocket faked a shot a couple of metres in from the top of the circle, then fired a high one to the short side. The puck glanced off the post and ricocheted in. After his three hops, he added a fist in the air. Two goals, back-to-back, on breakaways, he was totally pumped. He skated past the Toros centre, who was cruising back, his stick across his knees.

"I'll keep doing that until you say sorry," Rocket said to him.

The centre grimaced. "Big talk. You won't make it through the game."

Rocket laughed and held out his glove to Noah.

CHAPTER 20

Rocket leaned back against the dressing room wall. André was being nice, of course, and it was cool when a teammate appreciated one of his goals, but the captain needed to chill. He'd been talking about Rocket for the past two minutes.

"I loved the third goal the most," André said, for the second time. "You got by them like they weren't even there. The D was so cocky before that, too. No wonder they call you Rocket." He paused. "I googled you. They had a write-up on the Huskies website from last year. You were top scorer in the league."

"My last name is Rockwood, so that's where Rocket comes from . . ." he offered.

"And the shot. Bing! Off the crossbar! Awesome," André said.

"Feels good to win," Rocket said.

Coach Sonia entered. "I'll be fast, and then you guys can get dressed. We did well keeping the puck out of the slot in front of Dominic, and the D did a great job letting him see the pucks from the point. On offence, obviously it was nice to have four goals from

Bryan, but we can't count on that every game. We could do a lot better at controlling the puck in their end. You guys need to start using your size to cycle down low. We'll work on it at Wednesday's practice."

"But it's a big win, boys. They're a good team; they beat us five times last season. Four to two is a great result. Remember we have a tournament next weekend. I've sent your parents an email with all the details. It's kind of last minute, but the tourney I was interested in folded up and I want to get one in before the break." She clapped a few times. "Nice win! Go Big Blue!" She flashed a thumbs-up and left.

"Hey, Rocket. How many did you get tonight?" Blake said.

Rocket knew he was being messed with. "Four," he said softly.

Blake counted on his hands. "Bro, that's all the goals we got."

Forgetting his shoulder pads, Rocket pulled off his sweater.

"You sure don't like to bulk up. Those pads from a museum?" Blake said.

So much for keeping them a secret. At least nobody had laughed. "I lost my real pair. I'll get new ones soon."

"If you keep scoring like that, I won't have to bother going on the ice," Blake said. "I could set my Xbox up on the bench."

"I'm up for that," Dominic said.

"Might need a goalie," Matthew offered.

Dominic responded with a cockeyed grin. "Rocket can rag the puck."

The boys laughed.

"Let him score ten first, and then you can get gaming," Reid said.

"Score twenty and we can all game," Andrew said.

Rocket took his skates off. The guys were telling him something, and it was coming in loud and clear. They weren't impressed with The Rocket Show.

"You ever got four goals before?" a kid named Michel asked. He was a winger.

He had — a bunch of times in house league, and a few with the Huskies. "That was a weird game. Every time I shot, it went in."

"That wasn't luck," Blake said. "You smoked those dudes. It was fun to watch."

Now Rocket was confused. Blake sounded like he really meant it. Maybe he wasn't mad at him — maybe none of them were. They were all happy, talking to each other. No one seemed angry or jealous, like the guys on the Huskies would've been if he'd scored all the goals. Those guys would sulk if they didn't get on the power play.

He thought about what Blake had said: "It was fun to watch."

That was Blake's problem. Too much watching.

Rocket couldn't keep it in.

"You could've gotten a couple, easy," he said to Blake. "Our line, well, it has to play harder. Every puck is ours. Every puck. Let them get their own puck. We also weren't skating on every shift; sometimes we were standing still instead of meeting the puck at full speed. You'd be awesome out there if you went real hard. You got size and wheels and . . ."

The room had gone still. Not a sound. Rocket wanted to crawl into his bag. What a jerk. On the team for less than a week and here he was chewing Blake out in front of everyone.

A serious expression came over Blake's face. Rocket hadn't seen him look like that before.

"You're probably right," Blake said. "I . . . played like garbage. Sorry, boys. I couldn't get going. Don't know why. Didn't have my head in it."

"Me, neither," Noah said. "I didn't take it as seriously as I should have. This tournament I'm going for it."

Rocket hadn't wanted to kill the mood, but maybe this moment was good for the Blues. If the Toros were a decent AA team, then Rocket was convinced the Blues could at least compete this season. Maybe they could even win a few games against the weaker teams and squeak into the playoffs. The question was, did they want it enough to make it happen?

"I swear, this weekend will be different for me, too," Blake said. "I'm starting to get it from watching Bryan play like he does every shift. We can pick it up, all of us, every shift. We do that and we'll win some games."

The boys all started talking at once.

Griffen had warned Rocket not to take too long. Again, he was the first one dressed.

"Looking forward to the tourney, boys. See you at practice," he said.

Everyone gave him a nice goodbye.

Coach Sonia was talking to a parent in the hall. When she noticed him, she patted the woman on the arm, and waved to him. The other woman walked away.

"The team played well," Rocket said to her.

"It did. It did, indeed," she said, nodding slowly. "I wanted to ask if you were getting to know your teammates."

"It's only been a practice and a game," he said.

"If you have any problems, you let me know. Okay? It's not easy being the only new kid on a team that's been together for a while. I've been there, and I know how tough it is."

"I will. Thanks. Everything's good." He tapped his stick on the ground a couple of times. He could see Griffen through the glass doors.

"By the way, do you have a problem with your equipment? I noticed you've had two sets of shoulder pads, and neither seems very safe."

The obsession with his shoulder pads continued.

"I lost mine. These are temporary. I'm getting new ones."

"You don't need to," she said. "I have three kids in hockey. I have a ton of equipment at home — enough to open a store, I think. I keep wanting to give it away and never get around to it. My husband says it's because I don't want my kids to grow up."

"I'll be okay. Thanks, though." He could see Griffen glaring at him.

"Maybe I'll bring a pair for you to check out." She patted him on the back. "You did well, Bryan. Very strong skating this game, and I liked the tough defence, especially the blocked shot. That showed commitment. Good for the other guys to see that, too. See you at practice."

He said goodbye and pushed the doors open.

"About time," Griffen said to him. "I'm not spending any more time at a rink. Crappy coffee and the hot dog was rubber."

Rocket realized he'd forgotten to ask about a carpool again. It was too late now — Griffen had already pushed through the doors into the parking lot.

Maddy shook her fist at Griffen as they followed him out.

Rocket smiled at her, but it was going to be a long ride home.

CHAPTER 21

Rocket bounded up the stairs two at a time. At least the trivia team gave him something to do most lunches and sometimes even after school. This week they'd gone hard at it to prepare for the first match against Woburn. For some reason, he was totally pumped. He'd even begun spending hours on trivia sites. It turned out he actually had a good memory, and most things seemed to stick.

Megan had also taught him a memory trick. She'd said to turn words into images in his head, then imagine those images in familiar places. She called them memory palaces. He'd tried it — and it had worked!

He marched to the classroom and pushed open the door. It was empty. Maybe the meeting had been cancelled? They hadn't said anything on the announcements this morning.

Now what to do? He couldn't stomach another lunch in the library. He'd heard about an Ultimate Frisbee game in the field, but that was out. Kinger and the crew would likely be there.

Rocket turned to leave and almost ran headlong into Des. Rocket felt a weight lift off his shoulders.

"Not like you guys to be late," he said.

"Late? We're waiting for you," Des said.

"Did we move?"

"We have a floor hockey game," Des said. "I sent you a message."

"I forgot to check."

"You're playing, right?" Des sounded worried.

"I . . . umm . . . I could if you wanted."

"Great! Come on. Game's starting. Nigel says you're awesome, and we need some awesome, believe me. It's been a dream of ours to score a goal. Maybe you can set me up."

Des took off down the hall before Rocket could reply.

"I forgot you had a team," Rocket said, as he scrambled after him.

"We're the Organians," Des said.

"What's an Organian?"

Des looked like aliens had just landed in front of them. "You're kidding, right?"

"Let's assume I'm not," Rocket deadpanned.

"The Organians. It's a classic *Star Trek* episode, from the original series. The Organians are made of pure energy, but they take the form of humans to be nice to the Klingons, who think they're taking over the Organians' world, but of course they can't because the Organians are way more advanced, and there's going to be a war between the Federation and the Klingons until . . ."

Rocket held up his hand. "I'll download it. Sounds . . . awesome."

"Next to *The Trouble with Tribbles*, it's the best episode," Des said.

If Adam or Kinger found out Rocket was on the

Organians, he'd be labelled a geek forever.

He decided to play just this once, keep it low-key, and then he'd tell the guys he couldn't play anymore. He'd make up some excuse, like he'd hurt his knee.

Bird, outfitted in goalie pads, gave a cheer as Rocket walked into the gym. Nigel was in front of the net, on defence, and Daniel was up at centre, opposite Kinger.

This was going to be bad.

"Go Organians!" Megan cheered from the corner.

Kinger folded his arms on the butt-end of his stick. "Check it out, boys. The Orga . . . The Organisms have picked up a free agent. Got the extra-mini version, though."

"Here's your stick," Des said, holding it out to Rocket. "What's the strategy?"

"Harry, listen up," Kinger said. "The professor's about to teach."

Harry folded his arms on top of his stick like Kinger.

The sight of those two grinning apes made Rocket's blood boil.

"Strategy is, we kick some butt," he said, looking at Ty and Adam.

Both boys looked away.

"Maybe we should forfeit?" Kinger said.

"Do what you want," Rocket said, snatching the stick from Des. He stomped over to centre and put his blade down.

"I'll . . . um . . . play defence with Nigel," Des said.

"You need a new nickname," Kinger mused. "You got anything, Ad-man?"

Adam silently took his spot on the wing.

Kinger shrugged. "I'll take care of the faceoff."

Then he raised a finger in the air. "But his Rocket thing doesn't work for me. I dub thee Pocket Rocket. That's more like it. That's what we got here, a little itty-bitty Pocket Rocket."

"We're playing floor hockey," Ty said. "Just, you know . . . no big deal."

"I know," Kinger said. "I'm just talking trash, right, Pocket Rocket? I'm not serious."

Rocket gripped his stick so hard his fingers burned.

"No big deal," he muttered. "Let's play already."

A kid wearing a ref's shirt that hung down to his knees came over with an orange puck. He looked like he was in grade five. "You're the Butt Kickers?" he asked Kinger.

Rocket braced himself

"We are the Butt Kickers!" the team chanted.

They did that before every game — Rocket's idea.

"You're the Organians?" he said to Rocket.

The gym was silent.

Rocket nodded.

"Love ya, Organia!" Megan cried.

The ref held the puck out.

"You two could be in the same class," Kinger said. "You're about the same height."

The puck dropped. Kinger took a swing at it. He could have saved himself the effort. Rocket had already drawn it back to Des — letting his top hand follow through to smack Kinger in the ribs.

Kinger didn't mind; he even joked about it.

"Pocket's got some jam," he said. "I'll give him that."

Rocket buttonhooked in the zone between Ty and Harry, and banged his stick. Des didn't look his way.

Instead, he whacked the puck at Ben, who caught it easily and laid it to the side of the net for Harry.

Ben put his arms over the crossbar, as if he were sunning himself on the beach.

Rocket took the slot. "Des, watch Ad-man — Adam," he said, and Des scurried over. "Back up D and watch the guy behind you," he said next. Kinger had been sneaking up the side, looking for a breakaway pass.

While Rocket organized his teammates, Harry waited nonchalantly behind the Butt Kickers net.

"Are you ready?" he said.

"Bring it," Rocket said.

Adam began to walk slowly toward him, and Rocket noticed Kinger hustling back to the Butt Kickers end. He almost laughed — the pick play! Did they really think he'd fall for it? He bent his knees and leaned on his stick pretending he suspected nothing. Sure enough, Adam suddenly broke into a run, just as Kinger came over to set up a pick on Rocket's right side. Harry took the puck out on Rocket's right and passed it over to Adam.

The Butt Kickers ran that play all the time. The pick stopped the forechecker from getting to Adam, so it was usually a clear, and easy, pass. Or it had been when Rocket was the guy taking the pass. Adam was a touch slow, and Kinger underestimated Rocket's speed. Rocket slipped past Kinger's pick before he got his feet set. Rocket cut sharply to his right and extended his stick. He heard Ty try to warn Harry. Too late!

The puck was in the net before Ben could take his arms off the crossbar.

Megan let out a whoop and began cheering like

crazy. "First goal of the season; first goal in two seasons. Long Live Organia!"

Rocket hoped she would lay off the Organia stuff — definitely not helping his rep.

Kinger banged his stick on the floor. "C'mon, Harry. You're supposed to pass to our team."

Harry gave Kinger a dark look and kicked at the floor.

"Doesn't matter," Adam said. "Let's stop messing around and get it back."

Rocket's teammates, looks of disbelief on their faces, held their hands in the air. Embarrassed just by being here, the last thing Rocket wanted was a big celebration, but he slapped their hands to be polite.

"I'm taking the draw," Rocket heard Ty say. He set up at centre, and he didn't look too happy.

Rocket decided to make a joke about the goal. "Thanks for the gift," he said. "Bet it'll be my last against you guys."

Ty relaxed his stance and looked up. "Dumb pass. You made a good play."

Rocket put his blade down. He and Ty used to practise faceoffs for hours in Ty's basement, with his little brother as ref. Ty was good, but Rocket won most of the time.

Rocket figured Ty would play it straight and go for the backhand sweep, so he stayed with the forehand. When the puck dropped, he jammed Ty's stick and used his right foot to kick the puck back to Nigel. Ty slid around Rocket to forecheck, with Adam covering Daniel wide right. Rocket turned and moved to his left a couple of metres, hoping for a pass. Nigel held the puck, looking right and left, then he did the worst possible thing by flinging it right at Ty.

Ty caught it with his hand and tossed it to the right, bursting to the outside. Rocket gave chase. Ty turned the corner, puck on his backhand, and pulled it across his body onto his forehand. Rocket dove stick-first and knocked the puck forward to Bird, who dropped on it. Rocket winced as he got up, his knees and elbows stinging.

Bird shook the puck in his glove. "You take it," he said to Rocket.

There were no faceoffs when a goalie froze the puck. The defending team took it from behind the net, usually one of the defencemen.

Rocket shook his head. "Daniel or Nigel should take it out," he said. "I need to go up."

"You can take it," Daniel told Rocket. "I'll cover the front."

Rocket felt self-conscious. This was becoming a one-man team. His teammates stood around watching him. "Spread out, guys," he whispered.

Kinger's laugh echoed off the walls. "Don't be fooled," he said. "The Organisms only pretend not to have a clue."

Ty didn't so much as crack a smile — neither did Adam.

Bird dropped the puck behind the net to Rocket, which signalled that play was on. For an instant, no one moved, and then Ty and Adam came at him from opposite sides. Rocket's mind raced. He was going to be sandwiched, and there was no one to pass to. He figured he had only one play.

He waited until they were about two metres away, and then he flicked the puck onto his blade and jumped through the gap between Adam and the goalpost. Bird was so taken by surprise, he flopped to the floor in a butterfly. Des, Nigel and Daniel stared at Rocket as he slid the puck onto the floor.

"Go, Bryan, go!" Megan chanted.

"Play the body," Kinger growled, his stick forward and his right arm out to the side.

Rocket knew Kinger was only imitating a defence-man. He probably hadn't faced a one-on-one as a defence in his life. Rocket dangled the puck, then brought it back to his left foot and pretended to snap his wrists together, as if taking a shot. Kinger closed his legs and pressed his arms to his sides to block. Rocket had no intention of shooting, however. Standing straight up like that, Kinger couldn't move laterally, and Rocket slashed to his right and streaked past. He was in alone. Ben was set this time: he crouched deeply, his big glove held high. Rocket liked the look of his five-hole.

The puck squirted through and in. Ben looked up at the ceiling. Rocket let himself smile. The Butt Kickers would win, but 2–0 would be sweet while it lasted.

Kinger's stick smacked him on the thigh.

Rocket whirled. "Watch the slash, jerk."

Kinger's eyes flashed. Without a word he cross-checked Rocket in the chest, sending him flying to the floor. Rocket jumped to his feet, enraged. Kinger crossed his arms and laughed.

Rocket clenched his fists, wanting nothing more than to wipe that cocky grin off Kinger's face.

CHAPTER 22

Words were his only weapon. Fighting Kinger would be like fighting a mountain.

"You suck on so many levels, it hurts. If you're this useless at floor hockey, I can't imagine how much you suck on the ice," Rocket said.

"You're on the worst team in AA, big shot," Kinger mocked. "Hockey's not for midgets."

"Did I just score two goals, or are you blind, too?"

"You'd last two seconds on the ice with me."

"You can't hit what you can't catch."

"So you can skate. You ever go into the corners?"

"Bite me, loser. You're all talk. I know how you play. Cheap shots and garbage goals is all you're good for."

"Then do something about it," Kinger said. He took a very big step forward.

"Leave it alone," Ben said from his goal.

Rocket backed up. He couldn't help himself. Kinger snickered and rolled his eyes. "Check out the tough guy. Biggest flinch ever." Kinger stepped forward and straight-armed him in the shoulder. There was no turning back. Rocket knew he was going to get killed, but that would be way better than being labelled a wuss and a coward.

"Anytime, bro," Rocket said. "Bring it. Drop your stick already, so I can shut your stupid mouth."

Kinger let his stick drop from his hands.

Ty stepped in front of Rocket. "This is over," he said.

"Out of my way — I have to teach Pocket a lesson," Kinger said.

"I said it's done." Ty stared Kinger down. "It's a stupid floor hockey game. You're going mental over nothing."

"The midget talks and talks and talks. He needs to show respect," Kinger said.

"What about the slash to my leg?" Rocket said, moving next to Ty. "Where's your respect?"

"Let's forget about it," Ty said.

"Why should I?" Rocket said. "He makes a team because he's big, but he can't even skate." Rocket felt better for having said that in front of Ty and Adam.

"Hockey's a contact sport," Kinger said. "Deal with it."

"Shut up, guys," Ty said.

"You act like I'm the only guy who thinks he's a joke," Kinger said. "You and Ad-man both said there's no way he can play contact anymore. Admit it."

Ty hesitated, but only for a moment. "I'd have him on my team before you, any day," he said.

"You really think you can stop me?" Kinger said to Ty.

Rocket found it hard to breathe. Ty had stepped up, big time. Now it was his turn. Maybe they weren't such good friends anymore. Maybe all along it had been more about hockey. But they'd been teammates for three years, and teammates stood up for each other.

"It's cool, Ty," he said. "I'm not afraid. I'll deal with him." Rocket braced himself. This was going to be ugly.

Ty didn't budge. "Can't do that," he said.

Adam came over and stood next to Ty, and Ben and Thomas joined him.

"Isn't going to happen, bro. Forget it," Adam said.

Kinger held his arms up in the air. "Whatever. Butt Losers is more like it." He pointed at Rocket. "Open invitation to finish when your big brothers aren't around to fight your battles. C'mon, Harry. Let's space."

Harry looked around the gym, first at Kinger and then at Ty and Adam. He shrugged. "I'll . . . catch you later. I have to talk to Ty about something."

Kinger rolled his eyes again. "I knew this was a waste of time. I'll open the invitation to any of you. Just tell me when and where." He opened his arms wide again. "Anyone? Just like I figured. All tough talk." He pointed at Bird and the others at centre. "I don't suppose any of you Organisms want to drop the gloves with me?"

"What does that actually mean?" Bird said.

Kinger threw his head back and roared. "That was perfect, bro. Perfect. *What does that actually mean?*" he mimicked. "Priceless, or what?" He left the gym.

Rocket knew he should say something. The boys had just done him a serious solid. They knew he couldn't fight Kinger. But everything he thought of sounded lame. He stared at the floor.

"I'm serious," Bird said. "What did he mean?"

That broke them all up.

"Means he wanted to fight," Adam said.

Bird's jaw dropped. "Fight that guy? Do I look insane?"

Ty elbowed Rocket. "You are nuts. You know that, right?"

"I might've lost my temper," Rocket said. "I probably would've taken him, though."

Ty shook his head, but he was smiling, and so was Adam.

Mr. Brighton, a gym teacher, walked into the gym with the ref. The veins in his arms and neck showed through his skin, and his forehead was deeply lined. He was mad.

"Who were the boys involved in the fight?" he said.

The ref looked around. "He was one," he said, nodding at Rocket. "The guy from the other team isn't here. He was really big, way bigger than him."

Mr. Brighton lowered his head and raised his eyebrows. "Who was this other guy, Bryan?"

Kinger was a king-sized jerk, and Rocket would've loved to see him get in serious trouble. But he wasn't going to rat on him. No way. Hopefully, Brighton had played a little hockey in his time, and he'd let it slide.

"Bryan? Will you answer the question, please?"

Rocket smiled awkwardly. "There wasn't really a fight. It was just . . . we were fooling around. It's hockey; you know how it is."

Brighton rubbed his chin with his hand. "So Edward is lying?"

Rocket didn't want the kid to get in trouble. He'd

probably gotten scared when Rocket and Kinger had dropped their sticks and he'd run off to get a teacher.

"We had a little scrum in front of the net. No big deal."

Brighton's eyes narrowed. "Fine. Don't tell me. But until I know who that other person is, I think you've played your last game for the year — and that goes the same for both teams. So is anyone talking?"

The gym was silent.

"I will not tolerate fighting — ever," Brighton said. He looked around. "Do you understand?"

"Yes, Mr. Brighton," a few kids mumbled.

"Good. Game's over. Put the sticks and nets away and get ready for your next class." He folded his arms across his chest.

Ty and Adam took their sticks to the storage room. Rocket cast a confused look at Brighton and followed them to put his stick away.

"Don't blame me, Rockwood," Brighton called out. "You know better than to get into a fight — over floor hockey, for Pete's sake."

"So, is that what you call a little scrum?" Ty said to Rocket when he walked in.

Rocket laughed and tossed his stick into the garbage bin. "Maybe it was more like a tussle. Sorry about that. I can't believe Brighton kicked you guys out."

"Brighton's insane," Ty said. "We all know that. I'm not defending Kinger for what he did, but I'm not blabbing to Brighton, either."

"No chance," Adam said.

"You hanging around after school?" Ty said. "We're playing soccer."

Rocket had promised to hang with Maddy. But Ty was obviously trying to make up, and it would be nice to be friends again.

"Sure. Sounds cool. I'll come by. Is a certain someone playing?"

"Who cares?" Ty said. "No one messes with us, right?"

They used to say that whenever another team tried to push one of them around. It sounded funny now that Rocket didn't play for the Huskies. It was nice to hear, though.

"So, after school?" Adam said.

He nodded. Kinger wouldn't show, not after this.

"I'll speak to Brighton, too," Ty said. "He might give us a second chance once he's cooled down. And, maybe, you could come back and play with the Butt Kickers?"

"I was dumb to invite Kinger," Adam said. "Totally on me."

Rocket knew he was turning beet red. "Maybe. I'll . . . um . . . We'll see. We can figure it out after school."

"Cool. Bring it," Ty said.

"Always," Rocket said. He nodded at his former two best friends, and he wondered if things might go back to normal, at least outside of hockey. "See you later." He left the storage room.

Bird and the team, along with Megan, were gathered in the middle of the gym.

"I still say we won the game," Bird said, "which makes this our first win ever. Thanks, Bryan," he said.

"We've been kicked out of intramurals," Nigel said. "What's the point of him being on the trivia team now?"

Megan glared at Nigel. Bird, Des and Daniel were at a loss for words.

"Nigel means it's too bad Mr. Brighton did that — it would've been fun . . ." Megan said. Words seemed to fail her also.

He didn't need to hear more. Things were clear. His sports-trivia expertise was not really needed — and they already knew the names of Asian cities. They'd only wanted him to play on the Organians and help them win. He felt like a huge idiot: a little boy who'd been tricked by the big kids. "Good luck next week against Woburn," he said quietly.

"They didn't mean that . . ."

He walked away before Megan could finish. He didn't want them to see that he was actually upset. Somehow, the trivia team had become important to him, something to do that wasn't so hyper-competitive, like hockey, but that he was still good at. And maybe, for the first time in his life, he'd felt, at least a little, that there was more to his life than hockey. But he'd been pretty stupid to think he was actually on the team — as if he contributed — as if he would ever be more than a hockey player.

CHAPTER 23

Rocket bounced the tennis ball on the blade of his stick. "Hey, Maddy. Did you tell Griffen to meet us behind the building?"

She kicked a few loose rocks on the ground. "Yes, like you ordered. Still not sure why."

"I wanted to warm up with a few shots," he said. But the truth was that since Connor and his crew had jumped him, he didn't like hanging out in front.

Maddy knew him well enough to see through his excuse. Just like he knew her well enough to see that she was seriously mad at him.

He trapped the ball with his foot and balanced the stick on the tip of the blade with his right hand. "Sorry again about Tuesday. Ty and Adam invited me to play soccer and I couldn't be rude and say no. You know how things have been."

She twirled her hair in her fingers. "You said that already in your message."

"That was stupid of me. I should have apologized in person. Sorry."

"Yeah. You're busy."

She looked away.

This felt weird. Maddy was always in a good mood, and she never got mad at him, not really, not for very long. But they hadn't talked in days, and now it felt different between them. It didn't make a lot of sense. Sure, he'd ditched her after school, but it was only one time — and it wasn't like he didn't have a good reason.

He fired a shot off the wall and trapped it with his stick. Then, on a whim, he reached into his coat pocket and felt around. It was there.

"I was going to save this for an emergency," he said with a grin. He held out a hard candy in a wrapper. "How about I give this to you and you can pretend you don't hate me." He jiggled it in his palm.

Maddy smiled, but not in her usual way. "I don't want it. Thanks."

Rocket dropped it back into his pocket. She wasn't going to make this easy. He figured he'd tell her about his tussle with Kinger. "Did I tell you I got kicked out of intramurals — and off the trivia team?"

She kicked a few more rocks. "I don't remember."

"Well, I did. Got into a fight, with this jerk named Kinger, and Mr. Brighton, this uptight gym teacher, kicked me out 'cause I wouldn't squeal."

She didn't react.

"The trivia team didn't actually kick me off, but the only reason they wanted me on the team was to help them win a floor hockey game. Their team's called the Organians. Guess what that's from. You're going to die when I tell you."

"Dunno."

"I'll give you a clue — it's from an old TV show."

"Don't know."

"Okay. So guess who the Organians were playing?"

Maddy shrugged.

"Guess."

"No idea."

"I'll give you a clue."

He kicked his butt with the heel of his shoe.

She stared at him.

This was getting ridiculous. "You're a ball of fun tonight," he said. "We don't hang out one day after school and it's a crisis."

Girls could be such a pain.

"Sorry I'm not more excited about spending my night watching you play hockey," she said.

"Then don't go."

"How are you going to get there, genius? Griffen said if he has to go, so do I."

Rocket blasted another shot at the wall. If only his mom had a car. Then they wouldn't have to be nice to Griffen. Lately, he was always calling her and asking her to go for a drink.

Maddy turned her back on him.

Rocket kept shooting, harder and harder. With every shot, he got angrier at her and Griffen, and even his mom. The ball bounced off the wall and Rocket swung at it with his stick. It hit the heel and skidded under the garbage bin to the right.

"Perfect," he muttered. The bin always stunk. He dropped to a knee and looked under. The smell almost made him gag. The ball was stuck under the back corner. He slid into the crack between the building and the bin and reached under with his stick. The ball rolled out.

"I'll mess that punk up big time if I see him."

Rocket froze. That was Connor.

"He's a total loser. You'll waste him," Raja said.

Rocket closed his eyes tight. He couldn't leave Maddy to face them alone.

He opened his eyes and began to shuffle out from behind the bin, desperate to think of what he could say to sound tough.

Maddy slipped in next to him and put her finger to her lips. They both remained perfectly still.

"Hey, that hockey dude lives here," Connor said.

"You mean the squirt with the shoulder pads?" Raja said. "That was out front."

"Duh! I mean it was this building," Connor said.

"Yeah, yeah, I know: in front," Raja said.

Rocket heard the sound of a bouncing tennis ball.

Let them take his stupid tennis ball and go.

"Nice catch, klutz," Connor said.

"Throw it near me next time," Raja said.

"You mean right into your hands again?" Connor began laughing. "You're such a total moron. You couldn't catch a beach ball."

"You whipped it at me. You're the moron."

"Anyone want this Coke?" a girl yelled.

Rocket figured that was Tina, the girl who used to be Maddy's friend.

"Pour it on Raja's hands. Maybe he'll catch the ball, if it sticks to him," Connor said.

"Pour it into Connor's brain and maybe he won't be so stupid," Raja said.

"That doesn't even make sense," Connor said. "You really are a moron."

"Forget you," Raja said.

"Give me the Coke," Connor said.

Rocket strained to hear what was going on. He thought he heard someone walking away. He and Maddy exchanged glances. Her face was white as a sheet.

Something smashed over their heads, and he and Maddy ducked.

"Why'd you toss my Coke?" Tina said.

"I was finished." Connor's laugh sounded like a machine gun. It faded as he walked away.

Rocket waited until he couldn't hear their voices, and then he pulled on Maddy's shoulder. They shuffled out from behind the bin.

"My life sucks so bad it's ridiculous," Rocket fumed, wiping the Coke from his jacket and pants. Connor had thrown the open Coke at the bin and missed, and it had sprayed all over him. "I'm supposed to show up in the dressing room wearing a can of Coke? Great. That guy's such a loser he can't even hit a huge open bin from five metres away." He threw his hands up in the air. "Look at me. I'm covered in it."

"I kind of got hit, too," Maddy said.

"But I got a game."

"Poor Rocket — always poor Rocket."

"What's your problem? I said I was sorry about Tuesday and you're still freaking out about it days later. I've got enough to deal with. I got bounced from the Huskies, I'm playing on the worst team in AA, I've been banned from intramurals, and I was so desperate to do something at lunch that I joined the stupid trivia team, but they don't want me either. Now I'm head-to-toe in Coke . . ."

Maddy was crying.

His anger melted away. He'd never seen her cry before. "Hey, Mads. I'm just whining. Don't take me seriously. It's not that bad, I guess."

"You live in such a bubble world it's unbelievable!" Maddy yelled. "I have to live with an idiot who does nothing but yell at me and boss me around. I have to be in my room by ten, I'm not allowed to watch TV, and he's always telling me I'm stupid, that I'm a pain and that I'm not grateful enough to him for taking care of me . . ." She was sobbing. "Why did my mom run away and leave me? I mean, she ran away and left me here, with *him*! I kept thinking she'd come back, but it's been a year! She's such a . . ."

She stopped and tried to catch her breath. "I have no one to take care of me, and poor Rocket complains about playing floor hockey with the *Organians*. You're at some fancy school — and so what if your team's no good? I don't play on any teams. I don't do anything except deliver papers to give Griffen money. And the highlight of my day? Seeing the great Bryan 'the Rocket' Rockwood play hockey. And I get to do it covered in Coke — thrown by thugs who go to *my* crappy school. On *my* lunchtime, I have to worry about getting beat up. So what are you worried about again? The *trivia team*?"

Rocket was stunned. Maddy usually acted like the happiest kid in the world. He hadn't known things were that bad. Or maybe he hadn't really thought about it.

"I didn't know . . . things were like that. Or maybe I knew stuff was going on, but I didn't . . ." He stopped to think. He wasn't being honest. He'd assumed everything was okay because she never complained. Not like him; he complained about everything. "I've been a bad friend, haven't I?" he said softly. "I've been obsessed with the Huskies and hockey — and myself, of course. Like . . . there's Coke on you and . . . I'm sorry, Mads."

Almost without thinking, he put his arms around her and gave her a hug. "What should I do to help?"

Maddy began to cry harder, holding on to the back of his jacket with her fists. They'd never done more than high-five before. Soon she let go and wiped her eyes.

"You don't need to do anything," she said. "And thanks for saying that. Maybe that's all I really needed." Her lips slowly formed into a crooked smile. "Besides, you can't do much anyway — you can't even stay on the trivia team."

He figured that was her way of trying to change the subject. "Do we have time to get new clothes before Griffen rolls in?"

She checked her phone. "Probably not." Her crooked smile reappeared. "So what do you think of your mom's new boyfriend, anyway?"

"What are you talking about? She doesn't have a boyfriend."

"What do you call Griffen?"

"A jerk." His stomach tightened. "Wait. Are you serious? My mom and Griffen — together?"

She shrugged. "That's what Griffen said."

He certainly wasn't going to complain to Maddy about it, but whenever he thought his life couldn't suck any worse, it did!

A red car turned the corner and honked three times. The driver's window lowered.

"Hurry up, superstar," Griffen smirked. "I don't want to spend my night in a stupid hockey rink."

Rocket and Maddy went over.

Griffen turned to Rocket's mom who was in the passenger seat. "Wasn't he supposed to figure out a carpool? Why am I driving him to a game on Friday night? We could be getting a drink or something."

Rocket put his bag in the trunk, placed his stick between the seats as gently as possible, so Griffen wouldn't get mad, and got in the back seat next to Maddy.

His mom turned around to give him a smile. She looked pale and tired. "Hi, honey. How was school?"

"School was . . . school. Nothing happened."

"It never does. Kids never tell us anything, right?" she said cheerfully.

Rocket knew something was bothering her. The two most important people in his life were unhappy right now, on top of everything else.

"Smells like Coke in here," Griffen said. "Maddy, you wasting my money on junk food? All I do is pay for your crap, and all I get is laziness back. Like mother, like daughter."

He drove onto the street.

"I spilled a Coke on my pants," Rocket said. "I bought it with my money."

Griffen grunted. "No wonder you're like a metre tall, drinking crap all the time. This hockey is a stupid waste of time, if you ask me. You ever seen an NHL player? Average size is like six feet and two hundred-twenty pounds. What're you? Four feet and eighty pounds of nothing?" He chuckled to himself.

"He's only thirteen," Rocket's mom said.

"Whatever. Kid's a shrimp and this is a waste of time. We should be doing something fun, you and me, not driving to a rink," Griffen grumbled. "Anyway, I know a café near there. We can drop the kids off and get a coffee and then swing by when it's over."

"I'd like to see the game," his mom said.

"We'll see some of it, but it's Friday night, and I'm not going to spend it in a dumb rink. At the least I want a good coffee."

His mom didn't respond. Maddy was looking out the window. Rocket resigned himself to a very awkward ride. They drove the rest of the way in silence.

CHAPTER 24

The dressing room sounded more like a birthday party than a team getting ready for hockey. Guys were tossing tape around and laughing and talking away.

Rocket pulled his bag through the door and leaned his stick against the wall. André moved his stuff over. Rocket took a seat next to him.

"I still think it's unfair," Blake said.

"Totally is. No point playing," Reid said. "My dad's totally pissed."

"Coach is talking to the tournament organizers right now. We should get our money back at least," Michel said.

André gave Rocket's knee a tap. "The first division didn't get enough teams," André said. "The clowns running this tourney put two AAA teams in our division."

"These spring tournaments are dumb anyway," Dominic said. "Who wants to play hockey in May? I wore shorts to school today."

The boys began talking at once, outdoing each other about how much they didn't want to play.

"Does someone have a Coke?" Blake said, sniffing the air. "I could totally go for an ice cream float."

Rocket prayed André wouldn't smell his clothes. He quickly took them off and stuffed them under the bench.

André didn't seem interested in a Coke smell, though. "Guys, I don't want to sound like the coach and rag on anyone," he said, "but . . . C'mon. This isn't hockey talk. I mean, it doesn't have to be like last year. We can win some games — we've already won one. So what if there are AAA teams? We can at least make 'em work for it."

"Yeah, right," Blake said, grinning widely. "You ever seen a AAA team? Those dudes play eight times a week, and they're huge."

"Bryan, you played AAA," Noah said. "Will we get wiped out if we play them?"

All eyes turned to Rocket. "It would be a serious challenge. Depends on the team. I, uh, think we could be respectable." He hoped that would satisfy them.

He was wrong.

"See," André said. "Bryan thinks we can compete and he played AAA for . . . How many years was it?"

Not exactly what he wanted to be reminded of.

"Three," Rocket said.

"We'll go nuts and take it to them," André said. He was getting worked up. "Hockey's about effort, not how many times a week you play."

"You're cracked, bro," Blake said. "We'll get smoked."

André scowled and stuffed his foot into his skate. Rocket found himself liking the fiery captain. Unlike most of the guys on the Blues, he played with real intensity and it showed. In Rocket's opinion, he was every bit as good as any of the Huskies defencemen.

"We can compete, that's the main thing," Rocket heard himself saying. It came out by accident, almost like he'd been forced to speak. Something about what André said had gotten him worked up, also. "Those guys aren't such hot stuff, though they think they are. And, sure, they can play, at least some of them. Practising a lot does help, and maybe some teams have bigger guys. But the real difference between AAA and this team, from what I've seen is . . ."

He hesitated, not sure how his little speech was going over. Blake wasn't laughing anymore. Noah looked deadly serious. Dominic had stopped strapping on his pads. André gave him a nod. He obviously wanted him to go on.

"The real difference is how seriously they take it. It's just a different feeling in the dressing room, on the ice, on the bench. Everyone's more into it. You make a mistake: you hear it. You make the same mistake: you sit a shift. No joke. Guys fight for every puck. That's what my old coach used to tell us. Pretend there's a gun to your head and if you lose a battle for the puck, the gun goes off." He began tapping his shin pads. "Would we beat the best AAA team in the league? Probably not. But if we outwork them every shift, we could put a scare into them."

"What AAA teams are we playing, anyway?" Noah said.

"The Kings . . . and the Huskies," Reid said.

Rocket felt the energy drain from his body.

"Isn't that your old team?" Blake said to Rocket.

All he could manage was a nod. It was one thing to talk big in a dressing room. But the Huskies would kill them. The news seemed to depress everyone else, too. They all began to finish getting dressed. No one said much. Even Blake sat quietly, staring at the wall. It stayed like that for a while. Rocket was happy when the door opened and the coach came in.

Coach Sonia came over to him, carrying a white plastic bag. She leaned close to his ear. "Take this. No sense buying new," she said.

Then she stood up and gave her clipboard a whack. "My, my, we are a serious bunch," she said loudly. "I kind of like it. This is more what a dressing room should sound like before a game. Anyway, I know some of you are concerned about playing teams from a higher division. I spoke with the tournament organizers and they showed me where in the fine print it says they don't guarantee what level you play against. Of course, it was so small I could barely read it. But it was there, and that means we can't get our money back. At the same time, it's not about the money. That's gone. If you don't want to play, then we won't."

"We'll play," André said.

She looked around. "How does everyone else feel?"

Dominic sat back and slapped his pads. "I don't want to take my stuff off now," he said.

"Bad luck to get dressed and not play," Blake said. "It's like taking out a samurai sword and not drawing blood."

"Interesting analogy," Coach Sonia said. "But I'll take that as an indication that we play. Good. No reason we can't get some positive results and have some fun. Yeah? So listen." She walked over to the whiteboard and pulled a marker from her pocket. "I want to go over the breakout we practised on Wednesday," she said, and she began drawing X's and O's on the board.

CHAPTER 25

Rocket squirted water into his mouth, swirled it around and sent it flying onto the ice in a steady stream. He put the bottle back on the shelf and grabbed his stick. As pumped as he'd been last night in the dressing room, he was ten times more pumped this morning.

Last night they'd played the Penguins, a AA team that had finished high in the standings last season — and beaten them 4–1. If the Blues won this game against the Blackbirds, they'd have a chance to move into the playoff round. They were playing hard, down to the last man: total focus on the puck, tons of energy.

"We're where we want to be, boys," Coach Sonia urged. She'd been pacing up and down the bench like a tiger the entire game. "You're 0–0 in the third period against a solid team. We need to be smart with the puck in our end. We gave up a few chances with passes up the middle. No more. I want it up and off the wall if you have the slightest doubt about getting it out of our zone."

Matthew poked at the puck with one hand, sending

it around the boards to Dominic's right. The Blackbirds left-winger stopped it with his skate and curled back to his blue line, surveying the zone over his left shoulder. Rocket fought to control his nerves. He couldn't help it. Whenever he wasn't on the ice, he felt disaster was about to strike, especially when they were killing a penalty, like now. Michel had gotten two minutes for tripping: a cheap call, but that was life.

The Blues forwards shifted to the right to pressure the puck carrier. Suddenly, Rocket jumped to his feet.

"Behind you, Matt! Back up!" he screamed.

The Blackbirds centre had cut around the net and parked himself down low, close to the post to Dominic's right. As if the left-winger had heard Rocket, he slid a pass to his centre. His right-winger charged to the other post. Dominic came across in a butterfly and slammed his skate against the inside of the net. Andrew left the right-winger in front and lunged at the puck. Rocket's heart sank. The centre calmly passed between Andrew's skates and the wide-open right-winger just as calmly fired it into the gaping net. Dominic's left pad didn't come close.

Across the ice, Michel slammed the penalty box door shut and skated to the bench. The Blackbirds huddled around the goal scorer, patting his head and slapping his shin pads with their sticks. A dejected Dominic scooped the puck out of his net and backhanded it out of the Blues zone.

"Sorry, boys," Michel said on the bench. "Dumb penalty."

"We'll get it back," Coach Sonia said. "Keep playing our game. Let's turn up the heat. We haven't tested their goalie too much. Fire from anywhere: he'll be cold."

"Go Big Blue!" Rocket said to his linemates as they filed off of the bench.

Blake and Noah didn't look like they had much confidence. They just took their positions quietly. Rocket skated to the dot, his stick across his thighs.

"Let's put this away," the centre said to his team. "Enough fooling around. We have to face the Huskies this aft."

"We're playing like garbage," the goal scorer said. "C'mon, Black. One goal is pathetic."

"Let's do this, Black. Crush time," the right defenceman said.

They thought the Blues would roll over after the goal. Made sense. Every team in the league was used to beating the Blues. But that didn't make it easy to listen to, and Rocket wasn't giving up that easy.

The centre put his stick down and nodded to his right defenceman. Rocket went with a regular grip. Time to show the Blackbirds that he had a few tricks up his sleeve.

The ref dropped the puck. Rocket flicked the puck between the centre's skates. It spun on its end about two metres in front of the right defenceman. Rocket evaded the centre's attempt to hold him up and got to the puck first. The right defenceman lunged at it wildly. Rocket sliced the puck over his stick and it rolled into the Blackbirds' zone.

The left defenceman didn't have a chance. Just like that, Rocket was on a breakaway, cruising in at top speed — his first really good chance all game. He hesitated a half-step to get the puck to lie flat, and then he drove in on the net. The goalie was crouched deeply in his stance. Rocket faked a shot. The goalie didn't flinch. Fine, Rocket thought. Try this on for size. He let the puck fly. The goalie dropped instinctively into a butterfly. The puck sailed over his right shoulder, top shelf, stick side.

Rocket slapped the ice with his stick and hopped three times, then curled on his inside edges to let himself enjoy the moment. Maybe the centre would take the Blues more seriously after that. He looked over his shoulder at the scoreboard. Six minutes left and it was still tied. They could win this thing! He looked into the stands. Maddy and his mom were on their feet clapping. Griffen was reading a newspaper.

André put an arm around his shoulders. "That was awesome to watch, bro."

"We do that again," Rocket said, "and it's Go Big Blue!"

"I'm with ya," Blake said, laughing.

The rest of the shift ended without the Blues getting another good scoring chance, but they more than held their own, and for the most part had the Blackbirds on their heels in their own zone.

Rocket reached for some water and looked up at the coach. He was burning to get out there again and get the winner. Reid had the puck at the Blues blue line. He faked a pass to Michel, who was covered by a winger at centre, and then whirled and rifled the puck blindly cross ice to André.

Rocket jumped to his feet. The blind pass found a Blackbird stick, and two players went in alone on

Dominic. The puck ping-ponged back and forth until it ended up in the net — an easy goal.

"Bryan's line is up," Coach Sonia snapped. "Switch it."

She obviously had confidence in his line, which felt nice. She was putting them out to get the goal back. He desperately wanted to do it, not only for her but all the guys. They'd be stoked to even tie this game. Reid and André stood together a metre in from the blue line.

"Focus, bro," André said. "You have to play it safe with five minutes left."

"I lost the game," Reid said. He was clearly miserable about it.

Rocket couldn't help himself. Everybody messed up sometimes. "Forget the *blaming* stuff," he said to Reid, giving his shin pads a solid whack. "It never happened. It's over. Flush it. No big deal, anyway, because we're going to get it back quick. They'll coast now, sit back and try to protect the lead. We take over the game and fire away. What d'ya say?"

Reid's jaw jutted out and he nodded. André slapped both their shin pads. "He's right. I got no right to call you out, bro. Sorry. We'll get it back and laugh about it later."

Rocket approached the faceoff circle, his eyes fixed on the puck in the ref's hand. They needed this draw. The coach had put him out for a reason. He took a deep breath and put his stick down. Before the puck dropped the Blackbirds centre pushed forward and knocked Rocket's stick away.

"You have to call—"

The ref cut Rocket off. "Outside, Black. Wait till I drop it."

"But your hand moved . . ." the centre began, but then he dropped his head and skated to the right wing. He knew he'd messed up.

Against a winger, Rocket didn't try anything fancy. He went for the backhand draw, and the puck slid to Reid. The defender justified Rocket's faith by passing to André without hesitation. The captain pushed forward. The centre pressured and André bounced a pass off the wall to Noah, who dumped it in hard. It rolled around the net before the goalie could stop it. The Blackbirds left defenceman trapped it on the boards with his skate in the corner. Blake had taken off as soon as the puck went in. He didn't stop until he'd levelled the defence-man with a massive hit against the boards.

"Bring it!" Rocket yelled. He'd never seen Blake play so hard.

Blake jumped over the legs of the fallen defenceman and took the puck on his forehand. Rocket swerved to his left and Noah cut in from the right side. Blake looked at them both and, without warning, bulled his way toward the front of the net, kicking through the goalie's outstretched stick. The right defenceman lowered his shoulder. Rocket cringed. Blake was going to get creamed.

The crowd roared and Rocket threw his arms in the air. Blake had plowed through the check and roofed a backhander over the goalie's left shoulder.

"That's bringing it big time!" Rocket cried.

He joined Noah in the slot, reached up and put his arms around his wingers' shoulders. André and Reid piled on and they formed a huddle in front of the Black-birds net.

"Power move by the Blakester," André said. "We don't back down ever again."

"What's that loser AAA team called again?" Reid said.

"Who cares?" Blake said. "Let 'em worry about the Blues."

Rocket loved it. He exchanged a high-five with Blake and Noah and skated toward centre. A tap on the shin pads from André held him up.

"Assume we tie this game. Since we won our first game, and since the Huskies will beat the Blackbirds this afternoon — they'll be tired after playing us — all we have to do is tie the Huskies and we're in the playoff round," André said. His eyes were so bright and intense it looked like they would burst right out of his cage.

Tie the Huskies?

Rocket set up for the faceoff.

Why not?

CHAPTER 26

Rocket craned his neck to see if they were coming. It was a quarter after six. The sun was about to fall behind the condo. Griffen was late again. He was going to miss the start of the Huskies game!

The Blues had ended up tying the Blackbirds, and the Huskies had beaten the Blackbirds later that day, just like André had said. The Blues might actually have a chance at the playoffs.

The Huskies had beaten the Blackbirds 9–0, though. Could the Blues really tie them?

"I told him to come at six sharp," his mom muttered. She looked at her cellphone and brushed her hair back. "He's so unreliable. Every time it's the same. I'm going to have a heart attack one day." She looked up at the sky. "So where are you, Griffen?"

She scowled and crossed her arms. He could tell she was angry, really angry. Was it something more than Griffen coming late? She wasn't the kind of person to just lose it. It had to be something else.

A horrible thought popped into his head, and not for the first time. It had been torturing him for days, and it made him sick to think about it. Maybe, and he hoped desperately that he was wrong, but maybe his mom had become Griffen's girlfriend so he could get a lift to hockey.

"Have you had any luck with the other parents about a carpool, or even the occasional drive?" he asked.

"I haven't had a chance," she snapped. "Griffen took me to some awful place Friday night before you played the Penguins. He called it a café; I'd call it a scuzzy bar. He actually tried to order a drink — and he was driving! I couldn't believe it. We had a huge fight over it, and I missed the whole game and didn't have a chance to speak to anyone or your coach. I asked Griffen to speak to your coach this morning, but Mr. Can't Remember didn't remember. I wanted to speak to her before this game, but at this rate, I won't have time. Maybe after." She stamped her foot and glared at her cellphone.

"Griffen can be a difficult guy sometimes," he said.

"He can be a royal pain."

"Yeah. I guess." He dug out a small rock from the grass and began to stickhandle. "Maddy and I were kind of talking yesterday, before the game, when we were waiting for Griffen to pick us up." He fired the rock across the street. Whenever he had something serious to say, he got nervous and couldn't think of how to start. "She, I mean Maddy, she was saying that maybe, well not maybe, she was saying it, that you . . . anyway, like that you and Griffen . . ."

She put her phone in her purse. "Me and Griffen?"

"She said Griffen was your boyfriend," he said.

He was terrified of her answer, and he felt his body stiffen.

"Bryan, if I ever have a boyfriend, I promise you'll be the first to know."

"But Maddy?"

"She might have exaggerated the relationship."

"But Griffen told her, to her face, that you were his girlfriend."

She took a moment to consider that piece of info. "He did? Hmm. Perhaps he and I need to have a talk. This is awkward, though. He won't take it well, and his car is . . . useful."

"You don't have to be his girlfriend so I can get to hockey, Mom," he said.

She burst out laughing. "I'm not that dedicated to your hockey career, Bryan. Sorry to disappoint you. But I admit I'm nice to him because, until we work things out, it's easier. But don't worry. By September, when the season starts, we'll have it sorted out."

"There's something else, too — about Griffen. Maddy told me some stuff: about him and her, about how he treats her."

A pained look clouded his mom's face.

Rocket hesitated. Maddy might be angry if he told. On the other hand, she hadn't specifically told him not to, and he really needed to tell someone. He described their conversation and how bad things were for Maddy at home.

His mom didn't say anything at first. "She's a strong girl," she began finally, "but she's had so much to deal with in her life. I worry about her. She's mentioned a few things to me, too. Thanks for telling me, Bryan. I won't tell her that I know about your conversation. I knew things were bad, but never knew they were that bad. I'm going to think about this, okay?"

"Maybe she could stay with us?" he said. "She basically lives at our place anyway. She's like my sister."

"It's more complicated than that," she said. "She can't leave home yet. She's only fourteen."

"That's not fair."

"That's the law until she's sixteen."

"I don't think she'll last two more years with the guy. That's like torture."

"Poor Maddy." She took her phone out of her purse and sighed. "I'll try calling again."

"If you'd let me take the bus at night, I wouldn't have to wait for him," he said as she phoned, "and you wouldn't need to be . . . so nice to him."

"No answer." His mom stuffed the phone back in her purse. "I don't like you coming back alone late at night on the bus. Anyways, let's not worry about that now. We need to grab the bus, and we can take a taxi after that. He obviously forgot, or he's just being his typical selfish self."

A red car turned the corner, did a U-turn in front of the apartment and stopped in front of them. The driver's side window rolled down. Griffen leaned his head out and rolled his eyes. "Hurry up, Risa. I don't feel like wasting my entire Saturday night driving to another stupid game."

His mom took a few steps toward him, leaned down and then took a step back. "You've been drinking! You've got to be kidding. You're late, and then you show up drunk?"

"I had one beer, woman. Lay off the drama, and give me a break."

"I'm not putting Bryan in that car, and I'm certainly not getting in either. I'm not really comfortable with Maddy in there. And thanks for being twenty minutes late!"

Griffen's face twisted in anger. "I'm doing you a favour, and I have to take your grief? Don't think so. You're kind of missing the big picture."

"There's no picture to miss." She practically spat out each word. "Thanks for the offer, but I think Bryan and I can find our own way to the game."

"I'm so upset I don't get to see the mighty midget play hockey." Griffen laughed.

His mom let out an exasperated sigh. "Maddy, do you want to come with us?"

"She isn't going anywhere. She can do her home-work — and clean the apartment for once. She's such a slob; all kids are lazy."

His mom's eyes blazed. "Maddy? Do you want to come with us?"

"I said she's staying put."

Maddy opened the door. He spun sideways. "You step one foot on that pavement and you're outta my life forever. Don't forget, I don't actually have custody. I can go to the government any time I want and give you up, then it's into social services and foster families and group homes, and I don't care what else. So you mind me and close the door."

Rocket caught a glimpse of Maddy's face. She was pale as a ghost and there was a tear in her eye. She closed the door and Griffen smirked. Rocket wanted to smack that arrogant grin off his face.

Then he got the surprise of his life.

"You're the cruellest, most awful man I know!" his mom roared. "How dare you talk to Maddy like that? How dare you! I have half a mind to call social services myself and report you for abuse."

Griffen's cheeks turned bright red. He stared at her, and then he opened his door and got out. "You do that and you'll have so much trouble coming down on your head, you won't know what hit you, Miss Smarty Pants."

His mom didn't back down a centimetre. "I'd worry about my own head if I were you," she said. "You definitely do not want to get into a war with me. I work in social services, and I know a ton of cops. One word from me and you'll have twenty policemen lined up to see you. Who do you have on your side?"

Rocket had moved next to his mom. He had never seen her this mad. She put her hands on her hips and took a step forward. Griffen snorted and rolled his eyes. Then Rocket heard the car door crack open, and Maddy got out.

"Get back in that car!" Griffen roared.

"You come with us, dear," his mom said. "You'll stay at our place until we work things out."

"You can't do that. I decide what she does," Griffen said, his face even redder than before.

"Call social services," his mom said. "I want you to. Then a team of psychologists and social workers will ask you a million questions about whether you're a good guardian to Maddy, and they'll talk to everyone you know. I wonder what they'll think, especially after some of the people in this building talk to them."

Griffen sneered and stuck his face forward. "Enjoy her. I've been trying to get rid of her since that worthless mother of hers left. She's a worthless piece of junk, too — and you're welcome to her. Don't expect a penny from me. She's your responsibility now."

Maddy had turned to stone.

Griffen looked at Rocket. "Your mom's quite the firecracker, superstar," he said.

"And you're quite the jerk," Rocket said.

"The little mouth that roared," Griffen said sarcastically. "Have a good game. Maybe you can get me tickets when you're in the NHL." He hopped back in his car and slammed the door shut. "I want her crap out of my apartment tonight, otherwise I throw it on the street, hear me?" He closed his window and drove off.

Rocket felt a flash of heat pass through his body, leaving him cold and disoriented. Maddy still hadn't moved. He felt so sorry. He couldn't imagine what was going on in her head, how angry, how scared she was. Griffen wasn't her father, but he'd lived with Maddy for years, and to just drive off like that was brutal. What a piece of work.

"He's the worthless piece of junk," Rocket said to Maddy. "Don't listen to him."

A tear rolled down her cheek. His mom put her arm around Maddy's shoulders.

"We'll get your stuff tonight, and you'll stay with us," his mom said. "Things will be okay, trust me. I'm happy for you to move in. We'll need to deal with social services, but I don't think Griffen will put up much of a fuss."

"You don't have the room," she whispered, "and how are we going to pay for stuff and . . ." She let out a sob.

"You don't worry about that," his mom said. "I have some money tucked away for emergencies, and I think this qualifies. We'll get by. Right, Bryan?"

"Absolutely," Rocket said. He was so proud of his mom. "You can't live with that guy anymore. No way. It'll be fun. And I can tutor you in math and science and help with all your homework."

That brought a smile to Maddy's face.

Maddy wiped away her tears. "I'm sort of surprised you've actually heard of the word homework. That's a new development."

"Tell me about it," his mom said.

"Are you guys going to gang up on me all the time?" he said.

"Big time," Maddy said.

"Well, kids, I think that's enough drama for today — maybe for the year," his mom said. "If Bryan's going to actually play we'd better get a serious move on. Let's get to the bus stop."

Maddy gasped. "My student pass is in my room."

His mom laughed. "Money's not that tight, at least not yet. I can pay your fare."

"Thanks, Risa." Then Maddy started to cry again. His mom hugged her for a long time. They were both crying when they let go.

Maddy came over and gave Rocket a hug, too. "That's for being such a pain all the time," she said.

His mom gave him a hug next.

"Not to ruin the moment, but is this helping me get

to the game?" he said, with a lopsided grin.

"Please, let there be a parent who lives near us," his mom said, her eyes lifted to the sky.

They set off down the street as fast as Rocket could roll his bag.

CHAPTER 27

Rocket turned sideways and pushed into the dressing room, pulling his bag behind him.

"We'll go with Michel at centre between Blake and Noah," Coach Sonia was saying, "and then . . ."

Their eyes met.

"Sorry," Rocket said. He felt sick. The Zamboni was already on the ice. He'd never been late for a game, not like this. He'd be benched for sure, and maybe not even allowed to play. The guys would be totally mad at him, too, as they should be. He'd let them all down.

"The bus took forever," he said, looking down at the floor. "We called a taxi, but it's Saturday night and it never came. I'm sorry."

"Who cares about sorry," André said. "Get dressed, bro. We're playing your old team. We'll get smoked without you."

Rocket sat next to Michel by the door and unzipped his bag.

"Thank god you're here. I was going to have to play centre the whole game," Michel said.

"Why take a bus?" Reid said. "Your car break down?"

Rocket began throwing on his equipment. "We don't . . . My mom doesn't have a car, and the guy who was going to give us a lift . . . He didn't show. We waited, maybe too long, and then . . ." He stuffed his shin pads in his socks.

"We can deal with that after the game," Coach Sonia said. "Maybe one of the other parents can give you a lift when your friend isn't available."

"He's not my friend," Rocket said. He realized he'd said that too quickly. The coach looked at him closely.

"Don't worry. We'll figure it out," she said.

"We can give him a lift," André said. "Where do you live?"

He hated that question. "We're north — the north . . . the . . . umm . . . north part."

He was sounding like an idiot.

"Not totally sure where that is, but we might be able to do it," Matthew said. "We live north a bit, too."

"My dad would drive across the country to get you to a game," Blake said. "He's your biggest fan. He keeps telling me to play more like the new kid. I keep telling him that I would play like the new kid if I could play like the new kid."

The boys laughed. Rocket didn't like being the centre of attention, but at least they weren't talking about his neighbourhood. He pulled on his hockey pants and reached for his skates.

"We still have a minute or two before we have to go out," Coach Sonia said. "I don't want to slow you down, Bryan, but you know the Huskies pretty well, obviously. Any tips?"

Rocket tugged on his laces. The Huskies were a

solid team: three good lines, good goaltending, three sets of defence. They had speed and size, and they were well coached. They had one weakness, however. He hadn't seen it when he played for them. But he knew it now.

He knew it because he'd had the same weakness.

"They'll be totally overconfident. Everyone on that team thinks he's going to the NHL, that he's a superstar. But, the truth is, they really only have two superstars, Ty and Adam." He tightened his other skate. "Last year they were numbers six and twelve. They score most of the goals, and are always on the first power play. We shut them down, the other guys will panic, or at least wait for them to put the puck in the net. If we keep those two off the score sheet, we can give them a serious game. I mean it, too. Don't be intimidated. We can definitely give them a game. We have as much talent."

"Can we do more than just give them a game?" André said.

Rocket pulled his shoulder pads over his head and slipped his arms through the straps. "We might need a bit of luck for that," he said. He liked these guys too much to lie. "But if we catch them off guard, and I'm sure we will, and if we play harder than them, every shift, every minute, then maybe?"

The door opened. "Zamboni's off the ice," a parent said. "Other team's already out there."

Dominic and a few other guys got up.

"Hold on," André said. "We go out as a team." He nodded at Rocket.

Rocket put his elbow pads and sweater on. His hands were shaking slightly and that made him fumble his helmet snaps. After what felt like forever, he got them done up and he popped on his gloves. He punched them together. He'd never been more stoked for a game.

"Thanks, guys," he said, his heart racing. "Last game was good. This game needs to be totally amazing. We bring it every shift — every single shift. Go Big Blue!"

"Go Big Blue!" the boys answered.

Dominic gave his pads a bash with his paddle, and he waddled to the door.

"Let's do this," Blake said.

"Hard all game," Reid barked.

"Blues all the way," Michel said.

Rocket let the others go first. He had to, since he'd told André about his superstition. Besides, he'd made them wait; it only seemed fair. André held back, too. Rocket had a feeling he was about to be asked a difficult question.

"Do you really think we can compete, I mean for real?" André said.

"Between you and me, if the Huskies play as good as they can, we don't have much of a chance. But I know those guys, and I know they'll be trying fancy stuff, doing the extra pass, looking for the perfect play. If they play like that, we might keep it close."

"I have to be honest," André said, as they shuffled to the door. "I'm getting tired of being on a joke team. Last year was brutal." He pushed the door open.

"Why didn't you try out for another team, or move up? You could totally play AAA."

André made a sour face. "Can't bail on my buds.

Besides, we got talent this year." He tapped Rocket's shin pads.

Rocket knew André meant him, but he pretended not to understand. "There are lots of guys who can play. We'll get better with more effort."

André held his stick out to stop him. "I forgot to ask. Some of the guys were wondering if you go by Bryan, or . . . do you like Rocket better?"

Rocket shifted uneasily on his skates. "I don't know. Whatever. The guy on the Huskies I told you about, Adam, he gave me the nickname."

André grinned. "I think you're more of a Rocket kind of guy than a Bryan. I mean, what's a Bryan?"

Rocket had to laugh at the way he said it. "The Y is kind of lame, isn't it?"

Together they went to the door leading to the ice. Again, André held out his stick to stop him. "You ready for this?" he said.

Strange how connected Rocket felt to the Blues, and he'd only played with them for two weeks. Three years with the Huskies and it felt like a hundred years ago, as if it hadn't even happened.

"Bring it — for three periods," Rocket said.

He was so pumped, he felt like he could have jumped over the boards.

They punched gloves and Rocket stepped onto the ice. The next instant he was churning across the blue line. Out of the corner of his eye, he saw the Huskies' familiar white and gold visitor jerseys — and then Ty went by. Suddenly, he felt unsettled. It was easy to say "bring it," but not so easy to actually play the best AAA team in the city. As he cut behind the net, he looked up ice. Ty and Adam were standing together at their blue-line looking his way. They were obviously trying to catch his eye.

If the Blues were going to keep this close, they'd have to be on those two like glue, and if that was going to happen, he'd have to be the one to do it. This was no time to make friends. That could wait for after the game. He kept his head down and continued around the wall, holding his stick over his shoulders and swinging it from side to side to loosen up his back.

CHAPTER 28

Rocket readied himself for the drop of the puck. Ty and Adam were on the wings, with a kid named Luke at centre — Rocket's replacement. This was one faceoff he wanted to win.

"Hey, number eighteen. Ready to bring it?"

That was Ty.

Rocket laughed and tapped the ice with his stick. "No other way to play," he said.

"Good luck," Ty said.

"You, too," Rocket said. He nodded at Adam, and he nodded back. The referee blew his whistle and waved to both goalies, then held the puck over the dot. Rocket drifted closer, his eyes fixed on the ref's hand.

"Go, Huskies, go!" the parents behind the Huskies bench chanted.

Luke committed first, but a bit early. His timing was off, and Rocket was able to slap the puck to André. Then Rocket shifted to his right to box Luke out. André gave it to Reid, who moved forward a step and shot it off the boards toward Blake. The left-winger took the pass in stride and, after crossing the red line, fired it deep into Huskies territory. Noah powered in to fore-check.

Luke and Rocket skated along in tandem. Rocket considered veering off to create some space, but then he noticed Ty curl up high near the Huskies blue line to his left. The right defenceman was camped out down low in the corner. The left defenceman had the puck on the other side, with Noah pressuring. Rocket put on the brakes. He recognized the play. The left defence would wait until Noah got close, then he'd pass to his partner, and Ty would go up the middle for a breakaway pass. It was high risk, and you'd only do it this early in the game if you weren't very worried about giving up a turnover in your own end.

Rocket let himself smile as he darted to his left to cover Ty. This was good — the Huskies were playing it loose.

"Not fair," Ty said to him. "You know our plays."

"Have to make you work for it," Rocket said.

The left defence sent it to the right defence in the corner. Rocket stayed on Ty, and Blake pushed past to forecheck. That left the middle wide open for Luke. The defenceman sent a crisp pass onto his stick, the centre spun and motored up ice, and just like that, the puck cleared the zone. Rocket didn't mind, though.

Luke was tall and had a long reach, but his stride was a bit choppy, as if he were off balance all the time. Not a bad player, he just wasn't Ty or Adam.

Ragging the puck over the red line, Luke lofted a dump into André's corner. Adam steamed over the blue line. André got to it first and headed behind the net, Adam in close pursuit. As André passed the net, he backhanded the puck backward off the wall to a wide-open Reid. Rocket thrilled at seeing such a great play from his captain — it set the tone.

Suddenly, he felt a presence on his shoulder. He knew who it was. He would shadow Ty, but Ty would shadow him: a game of cat and mouse.

Without warning, Rocket cut to the left boards and then up ice, forcing Ty to work to keep up. Reid lugged the puck to the slot and then gave Noah a nice feed. Noah got over the red line and dumped it in. Again, Rocket stayed a step away from Ty, with Noah close to Adam's side. The defenceman gave the puck to Luke, and he skated it out. After that, the puck rattled in and out of the neutral zone, both teams scuffling for possession, until Luke got hold of a loose puck and sent it deep into the Blues zone. Ty headed off; Rocket figured he should do the same.

"That's a perfect shift," Rocket said to his linemates, patting them on the helmets. "It's all about six and twelve. Keep the puck off their sticks, and this will be interesting." He sat next to Blake. "You played great. I have a feeling Ty, he's number six, is going to be covering me all game, which means you should have more room to motor." He tapped Noah on the back. "Remember that one of us has to watch Adam; he's number twelve. He's got a huge shot, so if the puck lands on his blade, rush at him."

"Take it to them, Big Blue," André said. He clambered over the boards to the bench. Andrew jumped out to take his place. "These guys aren't so hot."

The boys were fired up, and Rocket fed off their energy for the rest of the period. Ty got the puck a few times, but Rocket or a teammate were usually there to stop him. Rocket knew the Huskies weren't exactly killing themselves, but the score was still 0–0 when the first period ended. He would never have believed it.

The Blues crowded around their bench as the buzzer sounded. "The second period will be huge," Rocket said, banging his stick on the ice. "They're going to start getting irritated by not scoring. Everyone's playing great, awesome. Let's get the energy level even higher."

"No penalties, either," André said. "We can't give them the man advantage."

"More pressure on their D," Blake said. "We're giving them way too much time. Let's hunt that puck down."

Rocket had expected Blake to make a joke. Obviously, Rocket wasn't the only guy who was into the game.

"We're beginning to get predictable in our zone," Coach Sonia added. "D, you can start to skate it out yourselves up the middle, especially on Bryan's shift when they're focused on him. Centres, you could try hanging up high if the D has room to manoeuvre, then cut wide to give them a target."

Rocket looked up at the scoreboard and caught himself actually thinking about winning this game. He knew that was crazy, but it was nice to think about, even for a moment. He looked behind the bench into the stands. His mom was talking to another woman, no doubt trying to work out a lift for him. She always seemed to be doing something for him — Maddy, too.

Maybe he was luckier than he'd thought.

CHAPTER 29

Rocket swept past Adam and Noah, poking the puck free of their skates. With a joy born of being free of his shadow, he curled sharply about a metre above the Blues blue line and began striding up ice.

Midway through the third period, still tied at zero, this felt like the first time he'd had some open ice. They'd been covering him pretty close, and he'd been focused on keeping tabs on Ty and Adam. The Huskies defence slowed at the red line, both looking right at him. Rocket saw Blake roaring up the left side. The defence didn't seem to care much about him. Rocket knew what he needed to do. He cut to his right to draw the defence that way, and then he rifled a saucer pass to Blake. His winger took the pass without losing a stride, just a metre from the blue line. The defence was caught off guard. Blake made the corner and took it hard to the net — until the ref whistled the play dead!

Rocket threw his head back and let his arms dangle by his sides. He used to have a problem with losing his temper with the refs; he'd gotten penalties for it, too. Coach Neilson had drilled that out of him, so now he contented himself with a questioning look, then headed to the faceoff dot.

Blake had other ideas.

"Are you blind? Brutal call," Blake yelled. He slapped the ice with his stick and it bounced in the air. "I was way onside."

"Line it up," the ref growled.

"Line up your eyes!" Blake thundered.

Rocket stepped in front of him. "Forget it. Dumb call. No big deal."

"Total fix is in," Blake spat. "Can't let the AAA team lose, can we?"

The ref made a T with his hands, pointed at Blake and skated to the penalty box. Seconds later, two minutes appeared under Home on the scoreboard. The blood drained from Blake's face.

"What the . . . ?" he sputtered.

"Unsportsmanlike conduct," Rocket said quietly. "Don't say another word or he'll give you a misconduct, and we'll really be messed."

"I was onside," Blake said.

"I know. Stupid call." He tapped Blake's shin pads. "We'll kill it. No sweat."

Blake skated slowly off the ice. Rocket felt bad for him; he'd been playing so intense, which was probably why blew up. Not the best time, though. He glanced at the coach. She stood with her arms crossed. He was going to have a chance at killing the penalty, at least. Noah came over.

"Any ideas?" he said.

"We have to be aggressive on the puck. Pressure the D and they'll cough it up," Rocket said. "We absolutely can't let them start passing it around. Watch for Adam at the top of the circle for the slapper. He's got a deadly shot."

"Got it," Noah said. "Let's get this done."

Rocket won the draw to André, who killed a few more seconds holding onto the puck before lofting it off the wall and down the ice. Rocket was closest, so he took up in the slot, watching the defenceman set up behind the net. He glanced over his shoulder. Ty was trolling in the neutral zone. Luke was coming back to help with the breakout. Adam hovered on the left side, watched warily by Noah. Luke took the puck and circled the net stick side. Rocket began to backpedal, not wanting to get caught by a quick pass, when he heard a loud whistle.

That was no referee. That was Ty. Rocket's mind raced. He'd probably snuck behind the Blues defence. Worst-case scenario. No time to sound a warning — Ty was deadly on a breakaway. As the puck left Luke's stick, Rocket sprang to his left and reached out his glove.

A shot of pain raced up his arm.

The puck had hit him right in the palm. That was the bad news. The good news was that he had the puck on his stick, only eight metres separating him and the goalie.

"Stupid," Luke yelled.

The spectators roared and they rose to their feet. Rocket barely heard anything. He took off to the net, the puck on his backhand. At the hash marks, he transferred the puck to his forehand, stutter-stepped, hesitated another half-step and then fired. The defenceman slammed into him and he fell.

The crowd roared even louder. The goalie dug the

puck out of his net. Rocket got to his knees and then slowly to his feet. Behind the Blues bench, the parents sat in stunned silence, mostly with their mouths open. Rocket didn't raise his stick or do his usual hops. He didn't want to give the Huskies a reason to get mad. Hopefully, they wouldn't care about a measly little goal and would continue at half-speed. Besides, it was a total gift goal.

Suddenly, the Blues parents erupted in a frenzy of cheering and clapping, exchanging high-fives and hugging each other. The boys on the bench pounded the boards and high-fived each other. Noah threw his arms around Rocket's neck.

"Huge goal, bro. Awesome. Wicked shot," he cried. "Wrister under the crossbar. The goalie didn't even move."

André and Reid put their arms around the two of them. Rocket was still worried about showing the Huskies up. "Just a goal, guys, and we got a penalty to kill," Rocket said. "No big deal."

They ignored him, and kept celebrating by punching gloves and tapping each other's helmets. The Blues parents were chanting, "Go Big Blue! Go Big Blue!"

The ref blew his whistle and held the puck over his head at centre. The Huskies had already lined up, and Rocket could see none of them looked too happy. So much for not waking them up.

Seven minutes left — a lifetime against a team like the Huskies.

Ty was at centre. Jerrett had taken his spot on right wing. Luke was on the bench talking to Barker. The Huskies coach was waving his hands in the air and pointing at the ice. Rocket couldn't hear him, but he could only imagine the grief Luke was getting.

Ty put his stick down, and Rocket did, too. The ref held the puck over the dot.

Seven minutes for a miracle!

CHAPTER 30

Though they'd been around the same height in grade four, Ty towered over Rocket now. Rocket looked like his little brother.

The puck fell. Rocket crossed sticks to prevent Ty from getting the puck and reached for it with his skate. It would've worked perfectly, except the puck bounced up and he missed it. Ty began to push hard, and Rocket felt himself give way. But he had a trick up his sleeve. He spun backward into Ty's chest and his hip banged into Ty's leg, shielding the puck.

André had crept forward and managed to reach in and pull the puck out of the fray. Two steps to his right, he found an opening and fired the puck the length of the ice. It bounced at the hash marks and the goalie had to be sharp. Only a last-second pad save stopped another goal. The Huskies parents let out a collective sigh of relief.

This time the defenceman brought the puck out from behind the net and hit Adam on the left boards with a crisp pass. Adam one-timed it to Ty, who was breaking up the side, but Rocket had stayed with him and he was forced to drop it back to Adam. Then Adam rifled it cross ice to Jerrett, who gave it back to his defenceman. A quick move allowed the defenceman to elude Noah's poke check and cross the red line at pace. He blasted it in deep. The puck circled the wall until Ty trapped it with his skates against the side wall. Rocket stepped into him and the puck dribbled free. Unfortunately, Adam got his stick on it first and sent it smartly around the back wall to the right point. It was a beautiful play, and Rocket groaned as he raced to the high slot to take his spot in the box.

"Set it up, Huskies!" a parent yelled.

"Lots of time! Don't panic!"

"Around the horn and in!"

Rocket drifted back a bit. He didn't like Ty setting up in the slot.

"I got him," André barked. "Watch the point."

Good advice. The right defenceman passed across to his partner, who immediately wound up. Rocket, angry at himself for leaving the guy wide open, threw his body to the ice to block the shot.

"That'll leave a bruise," he said to himself. The puck had nailed him on the side of the leg. No time to lie around, however, and he forced himself back up. Jerrett had the puck down low at the hash marks to Dominic's left.

"Get the puck on net. How many times do I have to tell you that?" Barker shrieked from the bench.

The Huskies left defenceman suddenly charged to the net. Rocket fought to keep him to the outside, and he managed to get his stick in front of him. Ty was fighting for position in front of Dominic. A flash of white and gold whizzed by. Rocket spun back to the point. Adam had the puck on his stick. How'd he forget about that play? Stupid. He was furious at himself for getting fooled so easily.

Adam raised his stick. Rocket gritted his teeth and once more threw himself on the ice, his legs extended.

The puck hit him just above the knee. His entire leg turned red hot, as if someone had jabbed him with a burning needle. He ignored the searing pain. The puck was within reach. He stretched his stick out and brought it toward his body, hopping to his knees.

Adam came over and shoved his stick under Rocket's shin pads, trying to knock the puck lose. Rocket forced himself to his feet, his leg still throbbing where he'd blocked the shot. Trying not to limp, Rocket corralled the puck and carried it to his left, Adam harassing him from behind.

Rocket lowered his left hand to get leverage for a backhander out of their zone, but Adam threw himself against the boards to prevent the clearance. Rocket was forced to carry it deeper into the corner; hopefully he could ring it around to Noah on the point. But then he realized Noah wasn't close enough to the boards. The puck would go to the Huskies defenceman.

He saw Ty leave his spot in front of the net and curl around to forecheck him. Rocket felt helpless. It was the worst spot to be in on a penalty kill: the puck deep in the corner and no way for him to clear it. But he had to do *something* with Ty barrelling toward him.

He heard a gasp from the crowd.

"Careful," André shouted.

Too late for that, Rocket thought. He slid the puck

between Ty's skates, only a stick length from the net. Then he swerved left, just in front of Dominic, to avoid Jerrett's attempted check. He wobbled on his edges, almost falling, but he finally regained his balance at the hash marks. Legs aching and his lungs screaming in pain, he needed a change.

"Get the puck!" Barker screamed from the bench. "Whose penalty is it? The kid is two feet tall. *Get him!*" He had one foot on the edge of the boards. His face was beet red, his eyes bulging. "Get him. *Now!*"

Adam came at Rocket from the right. He loved to plow guys over, and tired at the end of his shift, Rocket was vulnerable. With no time to dump it out, Rocket jumped, doing a 360 to avoid the hit. The crowd gasped again. Adam's shoulder brushed against him. He felt his feet slipping. If he turned the puck over now, it would end up in the Blues net.

The game had morphed into slow motion: it was like playing in thick syrup. The puck lay close to the boards. Adam skidded past him, then fell as he tried to spin around.

Rocket bounced on his skates.

He'd done it. He was in the clear, with nothing between him and the goalie but a sole defender. His legs energized instantly and the pain was gone. He would show Barker what a two-foot-tall player could do.

Ahead, the defenceman wiggled his butt to gain some speed. It seemed like an awkward move. Suddenly, the lights went on. This was the same guy who'd nailed him at the Huskies tryout! Like two gladiators, their eyes met.

Rocket pushed as hard as he could. The defenceman

turned and skated with his back to him.

For a moment, they were even. Rocket called on his body to give him more. He needed separation, or he'd get knocked down or poke-checked. By the red line, he'd gotten a half-metre lead. Rocket anticipated a desperation dive and knocked the puck ahead.

The next moment he was sliding on his side on the ice, winded. Instead of diving, the defenceman had sliced his stick under Rocket's skates.

Hopping over Rocket's body, the defenceman retrieved the puck, spun quickly and rifled a cross-ice pass to Adam camped out against the boards two metres from the blue line.

Rocket raised himself to one elbow. All his energy had been drained by the fall. He felt good, though. He'd drawn a penalty and killed a good chunk off Blake's. They'd be on the power play soon, and it would be their turn to try and get the winner.

Adam shovelled a quick pass to Ty who was breaking into the Blues zone. Jerrett poured in from the right side.

"Ref! Blow the whistle," Rocket yelled.

Ty dangled the puck in front of Reid, then flipped it to Jerrett on the right side. Jerrett slowed as André stood him up. Rocket got to his feet. Where was the penalty call? Was this really happening?

Jerrett slid the pass across the high slot to Adam, whose one-timer beat Dominic high to the glove side. All five Huskies threw their sticks in the air. Rocket stumbled toward the ref, sweat stinging his eyes, his chest heaving, his legs heavy and sore.

"What game are you watching?" he said. "You were

standing right there. That's called tripping — and you gave them a goal. That's even worse than the offside!" He slapped his stick on the ice.

The ref rolled his eyes. "I'm tired of this from your team," he said.

Rocket watched the ref skate to the scorekeeper. He leaned an arm on the edge of the boards and spoke to him, then touched his hands to his hips and skated back to Rocket.

"Number eighteen, take a rest in the box. That's a misconduct, so you get to watch the rest of the game. And if you speak to me like that again, I'll have you kicked out of the league," the ref said. He pointed to centre for a faceoff.

Rocket dropped his gloves to his sides and looked up at the ceiling. Like a selfish brat, he'd blown it. This could kill their chances of winning — with another power play, the Huskies might even get ahead. Why couldn't he have kept his stupid mouth closed? The great Rocket had to chirp at the ref and take a misconduct. The Blues parents watched in silence. Coach Sonia's head shook slowly from side to side. His team-mates were looking down at the ice.

They'd had a chance to tie the Huskies and advance to the playoff round, but he'd gone and taken the worst penalty in hockey with less than five minutes to go in the game.

Ashamed, he skated head down toward the box.

CHAPTER 31

At the buzzer, Rocket left the penalty box and closed the door slowly. The Huskies had poured in three goals, and he'd sat fidgeting, pacing and squirming the entire time. Final score was 4–1.

Rocket skated slowly to his end, watching his teammates smack Dominic on the pads and punch each other's gloves. They were obviously down; it had been so close until his penalty.

The two teams began to line up to shake hands. Rocket slid to the back of the line.

Adam reached out his hand. "Brutal call, bro," he said. "You almost pulled it off."

"Thanks," Rocket mumbled.

Money was next. "Awesome game," he said. "What're you doing playing AA?"

Rocket shook hands with the rest of his old teammates. Soon, he was almost at the end.

Ty took his hand and held on. "Did you have to make us look so bad? Bark-Breath almost had a heart attack, and he's going to scream at us for an hour when we get into the dressing room."

"You guys deserved the win," Rocket said. He knew Ty was only being nice. "I lost it."

"Don't blame yourself. That ref was a jerk. Everyone on the bench said it was a total penalty. Even Hunter, the guy who tripped you, admitted it."

"Hard to say that makes me feel better, but thanks. I'm kind of dreading going into our room, too. The boys are going to be mad."

Some of the guys were filing off the ice. Adam came over.

"Still think you should call some AAA teams," Ty said. "This is crazy. You can't play for these guys."

"You should be playing for us," Adam said. "Luke is worse than useless. Never passes when you're open, and when he does, it's always too late."

Rocket didn't want his Blues teammates to hear this. "I'm not sure about that. Maybe if I grew."

Ty and Adam looked uncomfortable, and he felt bad. Not their fault he got cut.

"Catch you later, boys," he said quickly. "Good luck with the rest of the tourney. I'm not sure if I can come tomorrow for the final. No ride . . ."

"We'll give you a lift," Ty said. "I'll message you."

"Yeah. Cool," Rocket said. "You boys better win, though."

"Bark-Breath will kill us if we don't." Ty grinned.

Rocket gave their shin pads a slap and headed to the door. Things would still be different with Ty and Adam, but he knew now that they could still be friends, even if they didn't play on the same team or at the same level. Even if he hadn't been cut this year, there was no way they would have kept playing on the same team and the same line forever. They would have moved on to different teams at some point — or maybe one of them would have stopped playing.

Rocket stepped off the ice. He couldn't imagine a time when he wouldn't play hockey, but the idea of not playing didn't seem so crazy now, not like it used to.

He stopped in front of the dressing room door. Here comes the guy who blew it, he thought as he pushed the door open.

"Hey, get ready," Blake said to him. "You, me and the ref are going out for burgers. He can teach us how to suck up to him."

Rocket sat beside Michel.

"The guy was a clown," André said. "How'd he call that offside?"

"Rocket gave me the perfect pass, and I was going to dangle the goalie and roof a backhander glove side, I swear. I had it all figured out," Blake said.

"You were going to trip over the faceoff circle," Noah said.

Blake laughed. "But I'd have fired a bullet as I was falling."

Coach Sonia came in. "Obviously, a disappointing finish," she said. "We learned an old lesson: you can't beat the refs. This won't be the last time a ref blows a call."

"Two calls," Blake said.

She nodded at him. "I'll grant you that. Anyway, this is no time for lectures. Lots of good things happened, and a couple of bad things that we'll have to deal with when the season starts. Matthew's mom was nice enough to make cupcakes for everyone, so help yourselves. There are drinks, courtesy of André's father. Now give yourselves a cheer for almost beating a AAA team."

The boys let out a rambunctious roar and began talking all at once. Matthew's mom began to hand out the cupcakes. Rocket wiped his blades with a rag and slid them into his bag.

"Hey, Rocket, what did you say to that moron?" André said.

He wished André would drop it, but he told him.

André snorted in disgust. "That's garbage. You're allowed to say something."

"It's not like you mouthed off like Blake," Reid said.

Blake laughed harder than anyone. "I just needed some attention. Sorry, guys. I'm neglected at home."

"Don't forget about next Saturday, boys," André said.

"Awesome."

"I won't."

"Better be food," Blake said, as he took a chomp out of a cupcake.

"Not for you." André grinned. "You've got an anger management problem."

"I only lose my temper when I'm hungry — or when a ref blows a call."

"Hey, Rocket. You're coming, right?" André said.

Rocket stared at him.

"You got my email, about watching the hockey game at my place?"

"I don't know, maybe my mom did? I'll have to work it out with her, about a drive and stuff. When is it again?"

"I'll send another," André said.

Rocket zipped his bag and stood up. It would take a long time to get home — three buses. He had to clear out. "See you guys next week, I hope."

"Take it easy."

"See ya."

"Good game."

"Yeah. Great goal."

He rolled his bag to the door and grabbed his stick. He took a deep breath and turned around. "Sorry for that penalty. I won't do it again. Stupid thing to do — and it cost us the game."

"No worries, bro."

"Ref's fault."

He nodded to them and left. On the Huskies, each guy competed with his teammates for ice time, a spot on the power play or the kill — everything was a huge competition. You could never relax. The Blues made him feel like he was a teammate. They knew he'd blown it by taking that penalty — and they were letting him know he was forgiven.

The pain of losing melted away, replaced by pride in how they'd stepped up and almost outplayed the Huskies. Not bad for the worst team in AA. This was one game he'd never forget.

CHAPTER 32

"Is there a Rocket in the house?"

Barker was leaning against the boards, a huge grin plastered across his face. He winked. Next to him, the Huskies manager, Rob Thompson, was wearing an equally big smile.

Rocket wasn't quite sure how to answer.

"You gave us quite a scare," Rob said. "To be honest, I think we got lucky. Hunter deserved a tripping penalty. I was impressed by your two-way game, too. You shut down Ty and Adam at the same time! How can one player shadow two guys? Tell me?" He laughed and elbowed Barker.

Rob was wrong. Noah had covered Adam. He wondered what these two wanted.

"Listen, Rocket," Barker said. "I'm a straight shooter. I tell it like it is. Ask anyone. That's just me. Like or lump it. I don't care. So when I tell ya I made a mistake cutting you, then you can believe it. Period. I blew it. Not proud of myself, but people make mistakes and I'm human. I didn't listen and made a judgment call based on your size. But here's something for you to think about." He paused and held his hand to his chest. "How can you measure the size of a boy's heart?" Barker nodded slowly, and he raised both eyebrows, as if he'd said something incredibly profound.

Rocket had to stop himself from rolling his eyes. That cliché was from the ice age.

"Straight out," Barker continued. "We want you back. I still can't believe I cut the leading scorer on the team — in the league, even. Am I the biggest idiot in the world?" He slapped Rob's shoulder and the two men laughed. "We have a couple more tourneys before the summer break, and I see you between Ty and Adam. Obviously, I can tell you're blown away, and I feel bad that I put you through this. I do — we all do. So what do you say?" He paused for a moment. "Rob, I swear the Rocket is speechless."

He wasn't really — more like angry. It felt like they were telling him to come back, like he didn't have a choice. "What about Luke? Where will he play?" he said.

Barker let the air seep slowly between his lips. "Luke will have to learn that the best players play — and guys like him watch. Let me tell ya, Rocket, we have huge plans for the Huskies. We're not only going to be the best in the league, we're going to be the best minor bantam team in the country. We're planning a trip to Europe, so heck, why not the best in the world?"

"Let's tell the boys right now," Rob said. "Come into the dressing room. Mitchell will be so excited to have you back — and everyone else, too. Let's do it."

Rocket looked over at the ice. The Zamboni had a final strip to finish up the middle. The boys for the next game were huddled by the doors, waiting to get on. Parents were walking around the boards to the stands behind the players' benches. Back on the Huskies? He should be pumped, ecstatic, over-the-top happy. This was what he'd dreamed of since that horrible moment when Huskies cut him.

Luke would be benched for practically the whole year, and Barker and Rob couldn't care less.

Then there was Coach Sonia and his Blues teammates, especially André. Maybe he was wrong, but somehow he felt the boys played harder because of him. They also treated him like he was important, like they really wanted him on the team — like they actually liked him.

The Zamboni stopped near the boards to drop the snow before getting off.

"Thanks for the offer," he said to Barker. He felt dazed and weak. "It's nice of you. But I signed with the Blues, and I don't think it would be right to quit on them. Maybe next season." Even as he spoke, a part of him couldn't believe he'd actually turned Barker down.

Barker's face grew hard and cold. He looked at Rob. "Is this kid actually telling me he'd rather play AA hockey with a bunch of losers? Seriously?"

Rob smiled and let out a short, nervous laugh. "I spoke with your coach, Bryan, a nice lady, for sure. She said she'd give you your release and wouldn't stand in your way, considering what a great opportunity this is for you. I admire your sense of loyalty. I know it's sudden. Why don't you take a day or two to decide?"

Barker scowled. "I'm not begging, here."

"Don't bother. I'm staying with the Blues," Rocket said looking into Barker's eyes.

Barker's lips twisted into a mocking smile. "Throw away the most amazing opportunity of your life? I don't get kids today. I guess I was right about you in the first place. Your heart's the same size as your body — tiny. I only want real hockey players on my team, and I don't see one in front of me."

"We don't need to get unpleasant," Rob said.

"I only play for real coaches," Rocket said, "and I don't see one in front of me."

Coach Sonia walked over.

"Congratulations, Bryan," she said. "I know this is what you wanted, and I'm happy for you."

"Yeah. *Congratulations, Bryan*," Barker said. "Have a good year." He walked off.

"Um, good luck," Rob said. "I'm sorry about all this and . . ." He seemed uncertain about what to say next, so with a wave, he turned and went into the lobby.

"I said no," Rocket said to Coach Sonia.

Her eyes widened.

"I signed with the Blues, and that's who I'm playing for. I'm done with the Huskies."

"I understand how you feel about getting cut," she said. "I'm not sure you're making the right decision, though. Is this your pride talking?" She put a hand on his shoulder. "It might be hard to get back to AAA. Do you really want to give that up? You're such a talent; I'm not sure AA will challenge you."

"I'm not giving up anything. I'm going to try to make the NHL — nothing's going to change that. If I'm good enough to make a AAA team next year, I will.

If I'm . . ." He gritted his teeth. "If I'm too small, then that's the way it is. I like the guys on this team, and I don't like Barker. No way I play for him."

"We're happy to have you, Bryan. You're an inspiration to the other boys, truly. I can already see the difference. I'll tell you what, I bet you'll make the NHL, too. Size is—"

"I know. You can't measure the size of a player's heart."

Coach Sonia laughed. "I hate that expression, too. I was going to say that size is important in hockey, but there's a place for a few special players who can be effective without relying on raw power. That's what I hope to teach you this season."

"I'm ready to learn."

André, Blake and Noah walked by.

"See you Saturday," André called out.

Rocket waved his stick. "Take it easy, guys. Good game."

"Get that temper under control," Blake said, and they all laughed. The three boys went into the lobby to look for their parents.

"So what's up for this summer?" Coach Sonia said.

"Not too much, mostly doing my training."

"Of course, training," she said, with a twinkle in her eye.

Had he sounded too intense there? He spotted his mom and waved. She came over with Maddy.

"Hey there, firecracker," Maddy said.

He rolled his eyes at her.

"Excuse me, Coach," his mom said. "We really need to get going. We'll miss the bus if we don't hustle."

Rocket clenched his fists. It hadn't occurred to him. He'd acted so tough with Barker and Rob, but by turning down the Huskies, he'd messed his mom up. He could've gotten rides from Ty and Adam again. Without Griffen, they'd be on the bus all the time, and that took way longer. Some of the Blues had offered to give him lifts, but what if they didn't live near him, or what if their parents didn't want to do it? He'd done it again — thought only about himself.

"I can't let you do that," the coach said. "I'll give you a lift. No problem. Just wait for Michel to come out."

Rocket hadn't realized Michel was her son. No one had mentioned it. On the Huskies, Money and Jerrett acted like they ran the team because of their dads.

"That's very kind," his mom said, "but we live quite far — in the north end. It's too inconvenient."

"Not at all, and don't worry about the season. We'll arrange lifts. A few kids live out there. We'll figure it out."

"I spoke to some parents . . ."

"It won't be a problem. I promise," Coach Sonia cut in.

"Okay, but today it's too late, I think. We can take the bus."

"Don't be silly. I insist. It'll take two hours by bus."

"We're fine."

"It's okay, really."

"Let her drive us, Mom," Rocket said. "I don't think she minds."

The two women burst out laughing.

"Okay, I'm dying to find out — what did you say to the ref?" Maddy said.

"Yeah, yeah," Rocket said. "I know: I'm an idiot, and I cost the team the game."

"You didn't," Coach Sonia said. "We wouldn't have been in the game without your play. Anyway, I'd rather this happen now than in the playoffs or something. Think of it as a lesson learned."

"Bryan can't learn," Maddy said. "Trust me, I've tried."

"I've changed," Rocket said.

Maddy smirked.

"I see Michel," the coach said. "We can get going."

As they passed through the lobby, Rocket saw Barker speaking to a few Huskies parents. Had he made the right decision? He'd probably never know for sure. He might have blown it, like Barker said; he might never get back to AAA. His hockey dreams could be over.

Still, in his heart he felt he'd done the right thing, even though he'd made the decision without thinking about his mom. He'd been loyal to his teammates, to his coach and to himself. Isn't that what it meant to be a real hockey player?

Maddy had taken his comment about changing as a joke. But he hadn't meant to be funny. He'd not only changed teams, he felt like he'd actually changed as a person. He'd never be the same type of player. He'd never take his spot on a team for granted, or put down players who weren't as good. And he was going to be a better friend: he wouldn't take Maddy for granted again, either.

The Rocket was back. Hopefully, a new and improved model.

CHAPTER 33

Rocket closed his locker and slung his backpack over his shoulder.

Today had been good. He'd hung with Ty and Adam at lunch, and neither of them had any time for Kinger. Things were, basically, back to normal — they even understood his decision not to come back to the Huskies.

Ty had invited him to dinner that night, but he'd said no. Maddy was still sad about what had happened with Griffen, even though she pretended that everything was fine. She needed him.

A hand grabbed his backpack.

"Not so fast, mister. Didn't you hear the announcements?" Megan pushed her hair back.

"Yeah, so?"

Her face clouded over. "The trivia team? We have our first match — against Woburn . . ."

Rocket fingered the strap of his backpack. "I think the Organians will survive without me."

"It's not a survival thing. Everyone feels bad about the floor hockey thing."

"You don't have to apologize," he said. "I should apologize to you. I can't blame the guys because . . . I was sort of using you, too."

Megan waited for him to explain himself.

"Well, I always used to eat lunch with the guys I played hockey with, and when I stopped playing hockey with them, we stopped hanging out for a while. So, I know this sounds lame, but I didn't have anything to do at lunch. Then you guys asked me to join the team, and I only came because at least it gave me something to do."

"Okay, so we're even." Megan grinned. "The point is, we have our first match against Woburn today and we'd like you to be there. We could still use you for sports, Bryan. Besides, you have to come."

"Why?" He waited for her answer. The truth was, he actually missed the team. Trivia was in his blood now — he was still studying at night and practising with online games, when Maddy wasn't making him do his homework.

Bird, Des, Daniel and Nigel came down the hall toward them.

"Bryan just asked me why he has to come with us to Woburn," Megan said.

The boys smiled and lined up in a row.

"What do you think of our awesome uniforms?" she asked Rocket.

Awesome was an interesting description. They were dark blue and bright purple — not his first choice. Each had something different printed on the front. Des had a date: April 5, 2063.

Rocket pointed. "What's with that?" he said.

"The date of first contact between Earth and alien

life, at least according to Star Trek history," Des answered, as if it were obvious.

Rocket nodded at Daniel's shirt.

"Ben Grimm?" Daniel said. "That's the Thing's real name. You know, from the Fantastic Four?"

"Right. Gotcha," Rocket said. "And you?" he said to Bird.

"You're going to kick yourself. You know this one," Bird said.

Rocket stared hard at his shirt. "Kilby and Noyce . . . Oh, they invented the silicon chip, right?" he exclaimed loudly.

They gave him a cheer.

Nigel's shirt had a bunch of symbols: Ἀτλαντὶς νῆσος.

"I'm not even going to try," Rocket said.

"It's Ancient Greek for the Island of Atlantis," Nigel said.

Rocket stared at him.

"The lost City of Atlantis?" Nigel said.

Rocket let it go and looked at Megan's shirt. "I don't think a clue would even help," he said.

"Movies are a specialty of mine," she said. "'I should have known you would be here' — the first line from the first Harry Potter movie."

Bird held up a T-shirt for Rocket. It had the number 1016 on it.

As if the team's sports expert wasn't going to put on that shirt: Wayne Gretzky's goal total — regular season and playoffs. You don't disrespect The Great One.

They began to walk to the staircase.

"We'd better hurry if we're going to catch the 3:48 bus," Des said.

234

"So put on your uniform," Megan said to Rocket. He slipped it over his head.

"You sure you want to wear that in school?" Nigel said.

"You have to wear the colours with pride," Rocket said.

Nigel laughed. "I noticed you were hanging out with your friends again. You playing hockey with them?"

"No, but we've worked things out," Rocket said.

The boys all nodded their heads. Megan looked at them.

"Boys are so weird, it's weird," she said.

"If boys are so weird, then what do you call a girl who hangs out with weird boys?" Bird said.

"I call her one fortunate lady," Megan laughed. She gave Rocket a nudge. "If you're such a good hockey player, you should give us a pep talk, like a real hockey coach would do."

"I don't think we need one," Rocket said. "We have everything we need: teamwork, passion, skill — and totally sick uniforms. The only thing missing is an equally sick team slogan."

"How about, 'Answer the questions before the other team'?" Bird said.

"Not bad," Rocket said.

"'We know more useless information than you'?" Nigel offered.

"Better," Rocket said.

"'Don't even pretend you know more about Star Trek than me,'" Des said.

"Best one yet, but not quite there," Rocket said.

They pushed open the front doors.

A little more than a month ago, he'd been the Huskies starting centre. He'd been the kid who wore his hockey jacket every day, thinking he was the coolest kid in school. A lot had changed since then, but he'd never been happier. It didn't mean things were perfect in his life. Maddy's future was uncertain, and money was tight. Griffen had left nasty phone messages on their answering machine. His neighbourhood was still dirty, and Connor and Raja were still lurking around. The carpool situation for the Blues was still not settled. There was no guarantee he'd ever get back to AAA.

And he was still short.

It was just that, for the first time he knew there was more to his life than hockey, and he liked it.

But it didn't mean he wasn't making the NHL!

"The best slogans are short and sweet," Rocket said. "So I'm going to boil it down to two words . . . *Bring it!*"